ROUGHING THE KICKER

EMILY SILVER

TRAVELIN' HOOSIER BOOKS

Flag on the Play

Roughing The Kicker

Definition: When a defensive player makes any contact with the punter, provided the defensive player hasn't touched the kicked ball before contact.

"Everyone clear on the rules of the game?"

"Why'd you bring me here, Gabby?" I hiss, my eyes shifting nervously around the room.

"Because you know Matt is going to be here. I want any face time I can get with him." Her blue eyes take on a dreamy look. She's been swooning over this guy for weeks. But I'm not much better as my eyes seek out Jackson.

Red Solo cup in hand, he's with Rachel. My eyes narrow. She's twirling her hair as she rests a hand on his arm, laughing at whatever he said. White-hot jealousy spikes through me.

"Are you ever going to woman up and tell him how you feel?" Gabby whispers in my ear. I've had a major crush on my next-door neighbor ever since he moved in right before school started.

"Shush." I swat her away as they start to move everyone into separate rooms.

"Why are we playing this game?"

"So people can make out with each other and then

have to guess who's who." The duh in Gabby's tone is implied.

A lead weight sinks in my stomach at the thought of someone else kissing Jackson. Yet the thought of telling him that I like him sends me running scared in the other direction. Every time I try to tell him how I feel, my belly knots and I feel like I might puke. Why is talking to boys so hard?

"Remember, no talking and only seven minutes. Once everyone has had a turn, we'll come back out and guess who kissed whom." The chipper tone in Rachel's voice has me cringing. I don't want to be here but came to support Gabby and her quest to finally ask out her crush. I wish I had that same opportunity.

We sit and wait as people come and go, my nerves amping up.

"Tenley, you're up."

"I don't have to go." I lick my lips, trying to slink back into the shadows.

"You have to." Rachel rolls her eyes at me. "We have an equal number of guys and girls, and if you don't, it'll be uneven."

"It'll be fine," Gabby reassures me, pushing me in the direction of the closet.

Deep breath.

I open and shut the closet door, twisting my hands together. I don't like coming to parties. It's not my thing. I'd much rather be at home hanging out with Gabby and watching a movie.

The door opens and shuts and I suck in a breath.

"Shit."

It's one word, but the hair on my arms stands on end.

It's Jackson. I'd know that voice anywhere. His hand hits my shoulder as he settles in the dark closet.

I don't know who came up with this version of seven minutes in heaven, but I'm thanking them now as a warm breath ghosts my cheek.

Turning my head, my lips ghost his, and nerves erupt in my stomach.

I'm freaking out. I'm kissing Jackson. The boy who moved in next door and won me over the first day of school.

My hands find his arms, resting there as his tongue slides into my mouth. I lean into him, his cologne almost overpowering as I breathe him in. It's hard to think as he takes over, his hands cupping my elbows.

Jackson knows what he's doing. I've never been kissed like this. Never been kissed ever, in fact. I let him have control as I try to keep up with each stroke of his tongue. My toes curl as he sucks on my lower lip.

I could get lost in Jackson.

A bang on the door jolts me back.

"Time's up. C'mon out, man, and then we'll send the next couple in."

I blow out a breath, wishing we had more time. Seven minutes wasn't nearly enough to get my fill of Jackson.

"You're a really good kisser," Jackson whispers.

I don't tell him it's me as he backs out of the dark space. My fingers trace my swollen lips, wanting to imprint every second of Jackson's lips on mine. I'm on fire right now, wanting to drag him back in and tell him it was me and never to stop.

Instead, my phone buzzes in my pocket.

MOM

You were supposed to be home twenty minutes ago, young lady…if you're not home in ten minutes, you're grounded for two weeks

"Crap." I type a quick text to Gabby letting her know I have to go home and hope there will be time later to talk to Jackson.

Because after that kiss?

I'm on cloud nine.

Chapter One

JACKSON

I feel alive.

With the sun high in the sky and the grass beneath my cleats, I've never felt more energized. The pulse of the teams thrums around the empty stadium.

It's the second day of training camp, and I couldn't be happier. The Mountain Lions are already looking good. We missed the playoffs last year, but that's making us hungrier for a win.

"Special teams, you're up!" the coach shouts.

The team from Vegas came down for a friendly matchup. Keyword being friendly, but they're one of our biggest rivals, full of dirty players, so even during camp, cheap shots are being thrown. Every time we come off the field, our coaches are yelling at us to play clean.

Grabbing my helmet, I jog out to where my guys are lining up. The field goals kiss the top of the stadium where the Rockies jump out to greet us. It's the best fucking stadium in the country.

Stepping back from where my long snapper crouches, I nod, ready to boot the ball between the uprights. I take a steadying breath, letting all the sounds of the game around me fade into the background.

The ball is snapped. One step. Two. My vision tunnels to the ball as I strike it. The second the ball leaves the ground, a linebacker rushes me. Our own lineman is trying to hold him back, but with a quick spin, all three hundred pounds of him slams into me and my extended leg as I'm coming back down to the ground.

A popping in my knee has me curling into the fetal position as I hit the turf.

"What the fuck, asshole?" I scream, clutching my leg to me.

My guys swarm him. If this were a real game, flags would be flying.

"What happened?" Darius, the team trainer, is cut there in a flash, kneeling beside me.

"It's my knee."

White-hot pain blasts through my entire leg.

Darius puts his hand on it to steady me and I scream again.

"I'm not kidding when I say it hurts." I shove my helmet off my head and wince through the pain. I grind the heels of my hands into my eyes, trying to stave off the agony that is roiling through me.

"Do you need a hand?" The sun is shaded as a body moves over me. Casting one eye open, Coach Brooks is standing above me.

"I thought this was supposed to be no contact." I turn my gaze to my line of guys now kneeling close by. They look sick.

"That'll be a conversation for later." I sit up. Coach kneels down beside me. "I want to get you looked at. Be a good patient for these guys, alright?"

"We'll take care of him." Darius waves at two guys to

come help. "Let's get you into the locker room, and we'll get an idea of what's wrong."

"You're in good hands, Fields."

Whatever it is, it won't be good. I try to breathe through the pain as two of the players from special teams help me up. It takes everything I have not to lose my lunch from the pain of hobbling toward the awaiting cart.

"Jackson. What happened out there?" The team doctor greets me as I settle onto the bench in the X-ray room.

"Fucking asshole from Vegas, that's what," I grumble.

He claps a hand on my shoulder, giving me a sympathetic stare. It doesn't help my mood. Nothing does. Not the quiet chatter between the trainer and doc, nor the hum of the machine as I lie still on the table.

"It looks like it's your MCL from what I see. I want to get more scans done at the hospital to make sure your ACL wasn't damaged."

"Fuck." I clasp my hands over my eyes, trying to ignore every thought that starts racing through my head.

Out for the season.

Injured reserve.

Free agent.

"MCL is better than your ACL, Jackson."

"Not when you're in a contract year."

Bitterness drips from my tone. This was supposed to be our year. *My year.* Denver's year to make it to the Super Bowl.

"MCL, even a severe tear can repair itself without surgery in eight weeks. We'll know more later, but stay optimistic, Jackson."

Easy for him to say.

"YOU ARE VERY LUCKY, MR. FIELDS." The doctor comes into the room, clipboard held at his side. "There's no damage to your ACL, so no surgery will be needed."

I blow out a breath, the tension easing in my chest. I look to my left and see my girlfriend, Rachel, scrolling through her phone.

"So what happens next?" I try to sit up more, but even the slightest movement hurts my leg.

"You'll need to keep all weight off the leg for the next few days. No walking, no moving around, nothing." His eyes shift to my girlfriend, still not paying any attention to anyone. Only her phone.

"And after that?" My hand flexes at my side, itching to do something. Anything but sit still for the next few days.

"After that, you'll need to meet with the team's doctors and staff for your rehab plan. They will handle everything from there. Do you have someone who can help you in the meantime?"

I glance over at Rachel, knowing this will go over about as well as a lead balloon.

"I'll figure something out."

"No weight-bearing at all. I mean it. Any deviation could set your rehab back, and we need you ready for the season. You've got the meanest kicking leg in the league, so you need to be ready."

"Thanks, doc." I extend a hand before he leaves the room.

"Hey Rach."

My call goes unanswered.

"Rachel."

Nothing. Absolute crickets.

"Damn it, Rachel!"

This time, her brown eyes swing up to meet mine. Annoyance lingers there. "What, J?"

I don't miss the bitchiness hidden in her tone. "Did you hear anything the doctor said?"

"Why would I need to? I don't know any of that medical lingo." She snaps her gum. It might as well be the snap of my patience, because with the way this day is going, I'm all out of fucks to give.

"I don't know, because I'll need your help these next couple of weeks? I can't put any weight on my leg," I repeat the doctor's orders back to her.

"And why do you need my help?"

I scrub a hand over my face, willing myself to stay calm.

"Because you're my girlfriend? I need your help." It's like I'm talking to a child.

Rachel sighs, letting out an annoyed tone. As if it's my fault that I got injured today and not that punk from Vegas's fault. What an asshole.

"You know I have a photoshoot in New York next week. I can't miss it. They're one of my biggest sponsors."

Ahh, yes. The life of a beauty influencer. I'll never understand what she does, and she understands football about as far as she can throw one.

"So you're just leaving me to fend for myself?" Anger sneaks its way into my voice.

"Why are you yelling at me? God, you can be so selfish."

Breath, Jackson, breathe.

It's not going to do anyone any good if I lose my cool with her. Right now, she's my only option, and I need her help.

Rachel stands, popping her hip out. She's gearing up for an argument, but at least I know how to head it off. We've only been together for thirteen years now.

"I need help getting home. Do you think you can at

least manage that?"

She rolls her eyes but doesn't fight me. I'll take the small wins where I can today.

It's hard to imagine what I saw in her all those years ago. One game of seven minutes in heaven and I was hooked on her. But now it's hard to remember the reasons why we fell in love. We're two strangers passing in the night.

Rachel waves a hand in my direction, designer purse in hand. "Is this going to take much longer, J? I have things that need to be done." I grind my teeth together, hating the way she calls me J.

"Do you think this is how I wanted my day to turn out? Knee injuries aren't a fucking joke, Rachel," I shout. I'm at my wit's end today. My knee is throbbing, and the person I should be able to depend on is annoyed with me.

Her eyes roll. "Stop being so dramatic. God, you're going to be a bear to live with." She picks up her purse and walks out of the room. "Call me when you're ready to be discharged. I'll see you at your place."

Fuck.

There is no way I'm going to last the next few weeks with Rachel. Especially if she has some event in New York. It means I'm all on my own now.

I'm stuck in a downward spiral. If I'm not careful, I could cause further damage to my knee that requires surgery.

The nurse comes back in, saying they want to get my knee stabilized before I'm discharged. Before my thoughts can drag me any further down, my phone vibrates on the table next to me.

And the one person that can turn this day around just did.

Tenley.

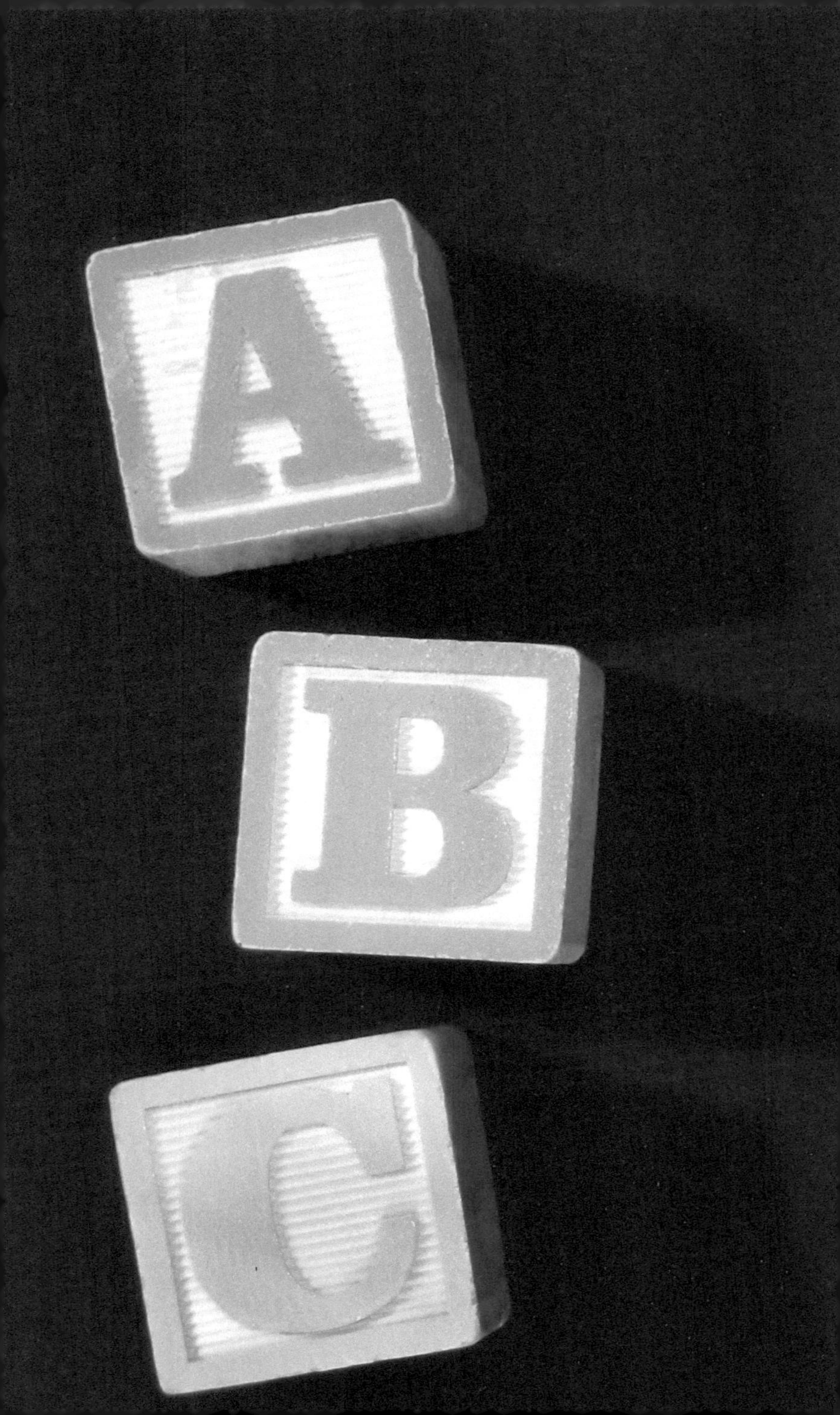

Chapter Two

"**I**t looks amazing, Tenley!"

Ashley stands behind me, clapping her hands as I wipe paint from my brow. The blooming tree on the wall is one of my better murals, if I do say so myself.

"Yeah?" It's still a few weeks before school starts, and I always like to paint something new on the plain brick wall in my class. One of the perks of being in a private school.

"The kids will love it."

"I can't believe the school year is almost here." I look around my empty classroom. It feels lonely without the voices of kindergartners floating around.

"I'm nervous," Ashley confesses. "What if they don't like me?"

My gaze moves to my new assistant. With her big doe eyes and a smile warmer than a summer day, I know the kids will love her. "Don't let them sense your fear, or they will steamroll you."

I didn't think it was possible for her eyes to get wider, but they do. "Oh God, they're going to eat me alive."

I throw my head back on a laugh. "You'll be fine. Just don't wear white pants and you'll be okay."

"Why not?" Her brows furrow together.

"My very first day of teaching, I had my whole outfit planned out. White pants and this top that had apples on it. I thought I was the epitome of a teacher." I laugh at the memory. It seems so long ago that I started teaching. "I never thought anything would happen, but during art time, one of the kids tripped and fell right into me. I had blue paint all down my legs for the rest of the day."

Ashley hides her smile behind her hand. "Okay, that's pretty funny. That won't be happening to me."

"See? Your first day will already be better than mine. I was mortified. And Principal Carson only laughed at me when she came down to see how I was doing."

Ashley stops laughing. "She's scary."

I shrug a shoulder. "You get used to her."

"I have so much to learn from you."

"You'll do great." I send her a wink. Checking my watch, I realize I'm now running late to meet my sisters for an early happy hour. "And a cocktail or two never hurts either."

"CHEERS to the start of a new year!" Penny, Nora, and I clink our glasses together.

"I can't believe that Tyler is going to be starting kindergarten this year," Nora wails. Tears gather in her eyes as Penny takes a big gulp from her margarita.

"I can't believe you're old enough to have a kindergartner!"

Nora, the middle sister of the three of us, started

popping out kids as soon as she and her husband got married. "My baby is all grown up."

"I wish he was in my class and I could see him every day." I dunk a chip in the salsa sitting on the table.

"And that's why I'm the favorite aunt. Because I get to pick him up from school." Penny gives me a smug smile, but I couldn't be unhappy for her if I tried.

"Someone's feeling upbeat." Only Nora could get away with calling her out like this. "Did you meet someone new?"

"Why can't I be happy just to be happy? I don't need a man to be happy." Penny pins her with a fierce glare. If it weren't for her light brown hair, everyone would think we're triplets. We look that much alike.

"You don't," I cut off Nora before she can say something that will get Penny riled up. "We just haven't seen you this happy since the divorce. And that makes us happy."

Penny rolls her eyes at us as she takes another glug of her margarita. "I figured it was time to stop wallowing and move on."

"Who are you and what have you done with our sister?" I say on a laugh.

"At least I'm not pining after someone I no longer have." Penny quirks a perfectly manicured brow in my direction. It used to make me confess all my secrets to her when I was younger. Now, not so much.

"I don't know what you're talking about." I glance around the brightly lit Mexican restaurant. The three of us have been coming here for who knows how long. Even with Nora now having three kids of her own, she still makes time for the two of us.

"Mmhmm." Now Nora is giving me a look. "How's Jackson doing?"

"Jackson's Jackson. Why do you ask?" I play it off.

They look at each other before looking at me. "Cut the crap, Tenley. You broke up with what's-his-face—"

I cut Nora off, "Ryan."

She waves a dismissive hand. "Whatever. You broke up with another guy. Why? He seemed perfectly nice."

"Excuse me if I didn't want to settle for perfectly nice."

"At least you were probably having sex on the regular." For the first time tonight, Penny's face falls. "God, I miss sex."

"You wouldn't if it was perfectly nice," I mutter under my breath.

"My point is, you need to stop pining after Jackson. He's never going to break things off with Rachel."

The mere mention of her name has my hackles rising. "I don't know why you two think I'm saving myself for Jackson."

"Oh sweetheart." Nora clasps her hand over mine. "You keep pretending like you aren't, but we all know the truth."

"You don't have to be so patronizing." I wave our waiter over for another round.

I love my sisters, I do, but times like these make me not like them very much.

"There's a new guy at my office. Maybe I can set you up with him?" Nora waggles her eyebrows at me.

"No." I point a defiant finger as a fresh drink is set in front of me. "The last guy you set me up with was still in love with his ex and cried the entire date."

"How was I supposed to know?" Nora gives me an innocent look.

"Clearly you're too loved up with your own husband to know the signs." I shake my head.

"You're right about that," Penny agrees.

Nora sips her own drink. "Maybe one of these days you'll find someone who can pull your attention away from him."

My phone chooses that very inconvenient time to buzz. I try to hide the smile spreading across my face, but I must do a poor job because those two read me like a book.

"Let me guess…Jackson?"

I ignore Nora and swipe my phone open. I hate that I'm so easy to read and that even though I try to hide my feelings for my best friend, I'm actually terrible at it.

My eyes fly over the message, my heart dropping to my feet. "Oh my God. He's in the hospital."

"What?!" They both shriek at the same time.

"I don't know. He just told me to meet him. Something about his knee? I need to go."

"Keep us posted?" Penny asks as I lean down to kiss her cheek.

"I will. Bye!"

I race out of the restaurant, my heart pounding.

Even the smallest thing happening to my best friend sends me into a tizzy.

Because no matter what I tell my sisters, I'm actually so far gone for my best friend, it's not even funny.

Chapter Three

TENLEY

"Hey, there she is!"

Jackson sounds drunk as I walk into his room. "Someone looks like they're feeling no pain."

He points a finger at me as I take a seat next to him. "They gave me a painkiller. Should wear off in a few hours."

The dopey grin on his face confirms this. "What happened?"

"Fucking Allen." He shakes his head. A heavy five o'clock shadow lines his jaw.

"Who's Allen?"

"Allen. From Vegas." Jackson says this like I should know who he's talking about.

"I don't know every football player. What'd he do?"

Shaking his head, Jackson pins me with a fierce stare. "We had a friendly game at training camp today. Thought it would show 'good inter-divisional camaraderie.' Asshole jumped off the line early and plowed into me. And boom." He motions toward his leg.

I wince. "What did the doctors say?"

Jackson gives me a lazy grin, showing me his pearly-white teeth. "MCL sprain. Out at least six weeks."

"I'm so sorry." I reach for him, squeezing his forearm. Even the slightest touch sends a zing through me. He's not mine, and I hate that my body reacts like this. Speaking of, I ask, "Where's Rachel?"

His jaw clenches. Whether in annoyance or pain, I don't know. "She had more important things to do. She should be at my place when I get discharged."

My own jaw grinds down in annoyance. Rachel. The bane of my existence. Jackson is way too good for her.

"Should be? Jackson, are you going to be able to take care of yourself?"

"Easy, tiger. I'll…manage." He forces the word out.

"Can you stay with your parents?"

He shakes his head. "They're in Europe right now. I think. Or maybe Asia. I'm not sure."

I smile. I've always loved Jackson's parents. As soon as they retired, they sold their house and have been traveling wherever they want. "I haven't seen them in ages."

"Probably the last time I saw them." Jackson shifts in the bed, a flash of pain distorting his handsome face.

"Are you okay?" I stand, wanting to ease his pain but not wanting to touch him and make it worse. For him or for me, I'm not sure.

His eyes are drawn shut. "It fucking hurts. Even with painkillers."

"What can I do to make it better?" I brush the loop of brown hair that fell into his eyes off his face. Chocolate eyes meet mine, causing my heart to stutter.

"You're here. You're doing it."

"Is it bad I want to slap the guy who did this to you?"

Jackson laughs. "Okay, Tenley. Sure you do."

"What?" I'm affronted. "It sucks that he gets away with this."

"Pretty sure the guys got into it with him. We'll get them back on the field."

"Football players." I don't hide the annoyance in my tone. "All so pig-headed."

Jackson's eyes start to drift shut. "It's a good thing you love me."

His words smack me in the face. He doesn't mean them. Not like I mean them. But it takes everything I have to still my face and show him that they don't affect me.

"You are my favorite football player." I punch his shoulder. We're friends, right? "So let me distract you."

I pull out my phone.

"How are you going to distract me?" He quirks a brow at me.

"Wordscapes."

The smile Jackson aims in my direction would bring me to my knees. But over the years, I've built a wall up around my heart. There are some cracks, but for the most part, it's done me well.

"Prepare to have your ass kicked, Rhodes."

"I can take you any day, Fields." I crack my knuckles and sit next to him on the bed. As I open the app, Jackson melts into my side. He smells like a hard day at the football field.

"I should get an advantage since I've had a bad day." Jackson sticks his lower lip out. It's a good thing I'm immune to pouts.

"That doesn't work on me with my kindergartners. Do you think it's going to work on you?"

Jackson laughs, nudging me with his shoulder. "It was worth a shot. You're too good at this game."

"I am one with the words. Now stop distracting me."

We settle into the game, our fingers wiping over the screen. Each word gets a victory shout.

But as the game goes on, and our competitive sides come out, my heart starts peeking over the wall. It's easy to be like this with Jackson. It's always been easy with him. When he first started dating Rachel, I was crushed. It was hard to be around them when they were in the lovey-dovey stage. But I've steeled myself against it over the years.

Having boyfriends always helped, even though Jackson hated every single one I brought around. It helped slot us into the defined roles of friends. Best friends. We've always been there for each other. I can't—*I won't*—abandon him in his hour of need.

"Ha! Nailed it!"

"Except that wasn't a word, you goofball."

"Yes it was—" he cuts himself off when it flashes at him. "Damn."

"Last person to get the word is the winner?" I ask.

"You're on."

It's always the hardest—the last word of the game. Concentration is the name of the game. So much so, that I completely miss the new person in the room.

"My, my. Don't we look awfully cozy."

Rachel's shrill voice has me jumping off the bed and away from Jackson. We weren't doing anything wrong, but my hackles always rise around her.

"I thought you were meeting me at my place," Jackson questions.

Rachel doesn't move her gaze from me. The piercing darkness in her eyes has always unsettled me. It irks me that I can't get a read on her.

"Aww, J. I felt bad about earlier so I figured I'd help you get home." The sweetness dripping from her voice has me backing away from them.

Tension rolls off Jackson the closer Rachel gets to him. "You told me you had to be in New York."

She waves him off. "That's a matter for another time, baby."

Oh God. I hate it when she calls him that. He's six feet one and weighs over two hundred pounds. He's anything but a baby.

"We don't need you anymore." Rachel waves a dismissive hand at me.

"Rach, can you not? Tenley was just being a good friend and distracting me from the pain."

Friend. If there's a word I hate more in the English language, I'll chew my own arm off.

"That's why I came back." She drags a manicured nail down his chest. "I'll help you."

Jackson's eyes flit to me. His face holds a look of regret.

"If you need anything, you know where to find me." Slinging my purse over my shoulder, I don't wait for an acknowledgment from them. "Take good care of him."

This gets Rachel's attention. She's so over the top, if she rolled her eyes any harder, they could roll out of her head. Casting one look back at Jackson, I make my exit. I don't need to be here when she's here.

It's a never-ending cycle. I know I'll never fill Rachel's role in Jackson's life. But every so often, I get a brief glimpse of what could've been. And that's always the most painful.

Because Jackson is exactly what I want in life.

But he will never be mine.

Chapter Four

JACKSON

"Rachel. Will you get me more ibuprofen?" I poke her sleeping body next to me.

It's late, almost three in the morning and the pain woke me up. The doctors stabilized my knee before I left the hospital. I was sent home with strict instructions not to move my leg. Any further damage and I might require surgery.

"Ugh, get it yourself." She flips to her other side, ignoring me.

"I can't get it myself."

"That's not my problem."

White-hot anger builds in my gut. It's too early to be having this discussion. My leg hurts, I'm tired, and I need something to take the edge off.

"You said you'd help. I literally cannot put any weight on my leg or it could do more harm."

"I didn't think it'd involve this." She throws the comforter off her and stalks off to the bathroom. I hear her rummaging around before she reappears. The bottle comes flying at my head and rolls off the bed.

"Seriously?"

"You're supposed to be good at catching footballs."

"I'm a kicker, Rach. Not a receiver."

She grabs the bottle and dumps two into my hand. "Is it going to be more of this? Because I need my beauty sleep if I'm going to look good for my shoot."

"The shoot in New York you said you weren't going to go to?"

"I never said I wasn't going to go." Long dark hair flips over her shoulder. "I can maybe put it off by a day or two, but it's important for me to be seen, J."

I motion to my busted leg. "And this isn't important? Dammit, Rachel, I need you."

"Sometimes we can't always be there for one another. I have my own life, Jackson."

Her words cut deep. I can't handle this right now. "Listen, if you can't be here for me right now, then we're done."

Rachel rolls her eyes. If I had a dollar for every time she did that, I'd be able to retire a wealthy man. "Stop being dramatic."

"I'm not being dramatic." I blow out a breath. Anxiety is building, my shoulders rising to meet my ears. "I just need someone I can rely on to help me, and right now, that person isn't you."

The bitterness in my words must get her attention. "Is this about Tenley?"

I swear, this woman gives me whiplash. "No. This isn't about Tenley. It's about you not being here for me when I need you. You're too busy worrying about your damn sponsors in New York to be able to help me! I'm done, Rachel. I just can't anymore."

"Okay." She spins on her heel and walks over to her overnight bag. It should've raised a red flag that I never asked her to move in with me. We were always perfectly content in our own space. If you love someone enough, you should want to be around them all the time, right?

"Okay? That's all you have to say?"

"We've been through this before. You get mad or I get mad, we break up, we get back together a month later."

"There won't be a next time, Rachel. I'm serious. We're done."

"Okay."

"Stop saying that!" I slap a hand over my eyes, frustration boiling out. It's been the longest fucking day, and this woman will not stop making it even harder.

"Fine, Jackson." God, that's even worse. "If this is what you want, then we're done. But don't come crying to me when you want me back. Because this?" She waves a hand over her lithe body. "This isn't yours anymore."

With a stomp out to the living room, I hear her shuffle around before the front door opens and closes.

"Fuck."

This day has gone from bad to worse, and I still can't make heads or tails of it. But the one thing I do know is I need help.

It hits me that the first thought after breaking up with Rachel—for good—is that I need help. Not that I'll miss her or that I have a deep sense of loss from her no longer being in my life.

It's like a weight has finally lifted from my chest. My eyes being opened to what our relationship actually was. Just the two of us together—neither of us needing or relying on one another.

We burned hot and heavy in high school. We couldn't keep our hands off one another. But gradually that faded. We went to different colleges. Saw each other only on weekends when we could. There was so much breaking up and making up that it made my head spin.

Now, there's a sigh of relief. The anxiety of getting through these next few weeks on my own won't be so hard if I can have someone reliable on my side.

And there's only one person I know who will do it for me.

Chapter Five

TENLEY

The phone cutting through my sleep startles me awake. It's just before six. Nothing good can ever come from a call this early.

"Hello?" My voice is sleepy.

"I need you." Jackson's voice is clear on the other end of the line. "I kicked Rachel out, and now I'm on my own and need some help."

I sit up, my sleep-fogged brain trying to process what he just told me. "What?"

"Look, I know it's early, but I need you, Tenley."

I'm up and out of bed without another word from him. "I'll be there soon."

Ending the call, I race around my small room throwing on whatever clothes I can find.

Jackson kicked Rachel out? Does that mean they're over? I try to quell the rising excitement in my belly. This has happened before. Rachel and Jackson fight all the time, break up, and then get back together. This doesn't mean anything.

Maybe if I keep telling myself that, I'll eventually start to believe it.

Grabbing my keys, I head out and make the familiar drive to Jackson's. It's one I've done hundreds of times over the years. And I love it because of the skyline coming to life in front of me.

Denver has always been my home. Will always be my home. There's something about the mountains rising up behind the city that brings me peace. Not that I'm overly outdoorsy, but they're a steady presence. Always there, never going anywhere.

Morning traffic isn't heavy. I make it to Jackson's high-rise in no time.

With each passing floor on the elevator, my nerves increase.

You're just helping Jackson. Best friend, no big deal.

Only he's the man you've been in love with since high school.

The warring thoughts do nothing to help the churning in my gut. The ding of the elevator has my palms sweaty as I slow my pace to Jackson's front door.

You can do this, Tenley. Kindergartners don't scare you, so Jackson shouldn't either.

Nerves steeled, I knock, waiting for a response.

"It's open." His voice is muffled through the heavy front door.

Walking inside, the apartment is dark. The sunlight breaking through the windows highlights the lump on the couch that is Jackson.

"How long have you been like this?" I drop my bag and stand over him. Brown hair points in every direction, as if he's been running his hands through it, trying to subdue the pain in his leg. His stubble is thicker than yesterday.

"A few hours. I didn't want to call you too early." He peeks one eye up at me.

I give him a soft smile. "I would've come at any time you called."

"You're a good friend, Tenley."

I hold back the wince. If I can't keep myself in check, Jackson certainly will.

"Now, what can I do for you?"

"Doc said ice and ibuprofen."

Clapping my hands, I head to the kitchen. "I'm on it."

The cold rush of air from the freezer cools my overheated skin. Being in proximity to Jackson always has this effect.

Finding what I need, I make my way back to the man in question.

"Okay, here's some ice. Hopefully this will help."

Jackson lets out a groan as I set the bag down on his knee. "Fuck. I do not recommend spraining your MCL. It hurts like a bitch."

"What else can I do to help?"

His face contorts in pain as I hold the cold bag still while he pops ibuprofen.

"Go back in time and tell whoever in the front office thought it'd be a good idea to hold a scrimmage with Vegas and tell them to fuck off?"

I roll my eyes. "Okay, maybe something I can actually do?"

"Rub my head?" Jackson purses his lips, looking more pathetic than I ever remember seeing him.

Giving him a soft smile, I round the couch—careful not to hit his leg—and lift his head. Jackson lets out a soft groan when my fingers swipe through his dark locks. I fight letting out my own at how soft and thick his hair is.

I've never touched Jackson like this. Intimately. Like he needs my touch for comfort. He's always had Rachel for this. But now I'm the one he's leaning into. Like he wants more.

"Did you know I didn't always want to be a kicker?" Jackson asks, peeking one eye open at me.

"What? Really?"

He nods. "QBs get all the glory. But then I remember walking home with you and Gabby one night, and she kept talking about that guy on the soccer team and I wanted to impress you."

"Why am I just now finding out about this?" A small laugh escapes, but it doesn't hide the shock in my voice.

He wanted to impress me?

"I didn't think it was that big of a deal. Besides, you started dating that dick not long after."

"Brad wasn't a dick." He was my boyfriend after Jackson started dating Rachel. I couldn't handle seeing the two of them together, so I jumped at the first guy who asked me out.

Jackson looks up at me, a knowing look in his eyes. "He stood you up for homecoming, Tenley. He got drunk and puked. That means he's a dick in my book."

"It wasn't all bad though." I smile at the memory. "I got to dance with you."

A small smile lifts one corner of Jackson's mouth. With his eyes shut, I get my fill of his handsome face. Thick eyebrows and eyelashes that kiss his cheeks. A smattering of freckles from being out in the sun. Dark stubble coating his jaw.

"I hate dancing."

I rest my hand on top of his head. "I know. And it was the best dance I had that night."

"Only for you."

My heart aches at his words. What would've happened

that night after our kiss in the closet if I hadn't had to go home? Would it have been me instead of Rachel all these years later? Would we have the same kind of relationship they had? One where we only tolerated each other?

The what-ifs are too many to think of. Because I'm happy that I've had Jackson in my life, even if only as a friend.

"Are you happy that you became a kicker then?" I ask, steering my thoughts back to more neutral territory. My hands keep drifting through his hair.

"Yeah. I actually have a pretty terrible arm and would have been cut if I tried to make it as a quarterback."

"And you lost out on all the glory," I jest.

Jackson opens his eyes, the full force of his dark brown eyes hitting me in the stomach. I could get lost in his eyes if I let myself. But I can't. Because I'm only his friend.

"I think I got my own glory in a different way."

"And how's that?"

"If I hadn't become a kicker, I don't think I would've ended up in Denver. I love being the hometown kid playing for the team he cheered for growing up."

"Do you ever worry about getting traded?" My hand stills on his head.

"Up until this year I didn't."

"Because of your knee?"

He nods. "I'm in a contract year. What if my backup comes in and does a better job than I did? I could be out faster than it takes the ink to dry on my trade papers."

"You're one of the most consistent kickers in the league. Denver would be crazy to trade you."

"I appreciate your confidence in me, Tenley, but it's still a business. If I'm not performing, they'd have every right to cut me."

I ignore the ache in my chest at the thought of him not

being in Denver. I know Jackson was lucky to be drafted by his hometown team. I love this place and have no intentions of ever moving. But the thought of being traded so callously because of an injury, despite years of loyalty, causes a sick feeling to settle in my stomach.

"Stop overthinking it."

"What?" I shrug my shoulders, even though his eyes are closed again.

"I know you. You can't imagine ever wanting to leave this place and how a team could cut you without a second thought."

"Am I that easy to read?" I laugh.

Jackson readjusts, draping an arm over my leg. Goose bumps break out over my skin at the warm contact. "We've only known each other half our lives."

"And yet, this is the first time I'm learning you wanted to be a quarterback."

"I think every little kid wants to be a quarterback growing up. Who wouldn't want to be Peyton Manning?"

"Think of all the hits you'd take as a quarterback. You might be out of the league at this point."

"I'm twenty-seven. I'd still have plenty of good years left if I played QB. But I'm happy where I'm at."

"I for one am glad you're a kicker. Way less worry for me every week. Although now I'm going to worry every time you play Vegas."

Jackson squeezes my knee, sending a rush of butterflies to my stomach. "They're known to be dirty players. I wouldn't worry too much about them."

"But I worry about you." The truth comes out in a rush. "And I always will."

"I'm glad I have you." Jackson gives me a warm smile. "In case I haven't said it before, thank you."

"You don't have to thank me for being your friend."

"I mean it. I can count on one hand the number of people who would drop everything to help me. And there's about four. And two of them are out of the country."

"How is your brother?"

"As you'd expect. Tired as hell chasing after a two-year-old, but loving every second of it."

"Do you think you'll ever have kids?"

"Going a little deep there, Tenley."

"It never came up with Rachel?" I gaze down at him, giving him a knowing glance.

Jackson huffs out a breath. "Never. She was too involved with herself to ever want to focus on anything else. And football has always been my biggest focus, so the discussion never had to happen."

"But if you could, would you?"

I don't know why I need to know the answer. But I hold my breath as I watch him mull it over.

"Maybe when football is over. After a few Super Bowl wins. But why worry about something so far into the future?"

It's like Jackson took a pin to whatever expectations I had. I'm his friend. I'll only ever be his friend. I don't know why being here with him and helping him would change his feelings toward me.

Friends only.

I need to get a hold on my feelings for Jackson and lock them up tight. Because there is no future with him. And the sooner I realize that and lock my heart up tight, the better off I'll be.

Friends only.

Now if I say it to myself a thousand more times, maybe I'll believe it.

Chapter Six

JACKSON

It's been the longest seven days of my life. Having to rely on someone else for every little thing has been making me crazy. Don't get me wrong, I'm grateful that Tenley has the time to come and help. But I don't want to have to rely on her.

And hopefully after meeting with the team doctors and PTs today, I might be able to start doing more.

"How long will your appointment be?"

Tenley shuts her car door with care. "You slamming the door isn't going to hurt my knee."

She winces. "I'm not taking any chances with you. Precious cargo."

I smile at her. "Shouldn't be more than an hour or two. Hopefully it's good news and I'll get some exercises I can start doing."

"And that's going to be safe?"

The city is bursting with life as we pull out of the underground garage and head toward the team's practice facility.

"Of course. They won't start me too early."

"How's the backup? I don't think I even know who he is?"

"Stevens. He's decent. Rookie."

I sneak a peek at Tenley as she drives. A small smile plays on her lips.

"So no chance he'd take over your starting position?"

"I didn't say that. I just need to make it through these next few weeks in one piece and I should be okay."

And a long few weeks it's going to be. In all the downtime I've had this past week, I've been researching the hell out of the best ways to rehab an MCL injury. It's going to hurt, that's for sure. I can't imagine doing it on my own.

And I hope to God that there aren't any setbacks.

"Call me when you're done?"

Tenley's voice pulls me from my wayward thoughts. It took next to no time at all to make it to the team facility.

"I will. Help me out of the car?" I bat my eyelashes at her, knowing I probably don't need to.

"No need to turn on the Jackson charm. It's not like you can do much on your own."

"Don't I know it."

Tenley rounds the car, and given her tiny stature, she struggles to get me out without jostling my leg.

"When did you get so heavy?" She huffs a breath as I settle my weight against her since I'm not used to the crutches.

"Probably all that milk I drank in college." I wink at her.

She barks out a laugh as we hobble into the facility. "I'm sure that was it."

"Jackson. How are you feeling?" The team doctor is waiting for us in the lobby.

"I mean, I've been better."

He claps me on the shoulder. "Well, let's go get a scan and see how things are looking."

"See ya soon," I say, my gaze drifting down to Tenley. She looks nervous.

"Yeah. I hope everything goes well."

She gives me a quick squeeze before heading back outside.

Following the doctor back to the training room, I feel like I'm being led to my execution.

"GOOD NEWS, JACKSON." Paige, the team PT, and the doctor come into the room. "You're making good progress. I'm turning you over to Paige, and she'll get you moving."

Paige pins me with a knowing look. "We're going to get started on a few strengthening exercises, but you need to not go overboard."

I blow out a breath, not realizing how badly I needed this news. "Good. That's really good news."

"I know it's hard staying off your leg, but you're doing the hard work. And there's a lot more to come."

A smile plays at the corner of my lips. If it were up to me, I probably would've hobbled around my apartment for the last week.

Tenley saw straight through me. Anytime I needed something, she was there. I couldn't lift a finger without her jumping up to help. Fuck, if it weren't for her, I'd probably have torn the damn ligament by this point.

"What exercises am I looking at doing?"

"You're going to need to sit on your couch or bed and just push your leg out and pull it back in." She indicates the move from where she's standing.

"I'm sorry, that's it?" I could do that in my sleep.

Paige shakes her head at me. "All you football players are the same. You think you're invincible. Your body is recovering. If you go balls to the wall, you're going to do more harm than good. Is that what you want?"

"No," I grumble, feeling properly chastised.

"Thought so." She moves over to me, keeping her hand on my knee. "Now, you're going to do ten in a set. Three sets only."

I keep my mouth shut, thinking how I can probably do more. But on the first extension, someone may as well have taken a hot poker to my knee.

"Fuck."

"Not so tough, are you?" Paige smirks at me.

"Why does this hurt so much?" I ask as I bring my leg back down.

"You still have nine more to go."

Each progressive move feels a tiny bit better, but damn. I can't remember the last time anything hurt this much. Sweat breaks out on my brow as I finish the first set.

"And two more of those?" I huff out a breath. You would think I'd just run five miles with how winded I sound.

"Yes. But spread them out throughout the day. I don't want you overdoing it."

The door to the room creaks open and Tenley's head pops in. "The doctor said I could come back. How are things going in here?"

Her bright voice is a balm. "Well, Paige here is going to kill me with simple leg extensions."

"Has he always been like this?" Paige ignores me and directs her attention to Tenley.

"Yes."

"No," I say at the same time.

"I have not," I mumble, mostly to myself.

"He's always been stubborn. It's why I'll be making sure he doesn't overdo it."

Paige introduces herself to Tenley. The two start talking like I'm not even in the room. Tenley's asking questions I don't even think to ask.

"So when is his next appointment? Does he need to do anything else besides this before then?"

Paige shakes her head at Tenley's question. "Just this. We'll set the follow-up for next week. If all is looking good then, we'll move into the weight room." Paige directs her attention back to me. "The guys are looking forward to seeing you back out there."

The first preseason game is this weekend. Starters never play more than a few series. It's more for the newbies to try and find their place on the team. For the first time in my professional career, I won't be suiting up with them. And it fucking sucks.

"Not as much as I am."

"Okay. We're done for today, but remember your exercises. Two more sets and that's it. Use the crutches and keep the brace on once you're done with the sets. Don't be stubborn and think you know more than me. Trust me; you don't."

Tenley fights a laugh as I grab my crutches. "I won't do anything stupid."

"I'll make sure of it," Tenley pipes up.

Grabbing the crutches, I follow Tenley out of the room and back outside. "Fuck. I feel like a newborn giraffe trying to walk with these fucking things."

They're uncomfortable. I have to bend one leg to be able to use them. Every step is shaky.

"Come here." Tenley stops, grabbing the crutch out of my way and draping her arm around my waist. As small as she is, it's easier to rest my weight on her. "That better?"

I look down at her, and for a second, I forget what's going on. Tenley's blue eyes are bright. There's the tiniest flecks of green in them. Funny how I never noticed that before.

Tenley's always been around. She's been in my life for as long as I can remember. Most of my memories from high school until now—she's been there.

So why am I just now noticing her eyes? Or how whenever she looks at me, her smile could light up the darkest day?

I shake the thoughts away. It's been a weird week, from getting injured to dumping Rachel. That must be it. Too much change and having to rely on someone is making my brain fuzzy.

Because it's Tenley.

My best friend.

And nothing would ever change that.

Not even errant thoughts about how beautiful she is.

Fuck.

This is going to be a long few weeks.

Chapter Seven

TENLEY

"Tenley?" Jackson's voice calls out to me as I push open the door, arms loaded down with groceries. I dropped him off after meeting with the team doctors to run to the store. I shouldn't have been surprised that he has no food.

"Just me." Walking into the living room, Jackson is tossing a tennis ball against the wall. "How's everything going here?"

"Did you know the cash register building has thirty-seven windows?"

"What in the world are you talking about?" I set the bag of groceries down on the kitchen island and circle back into the living room.

"From where I can see it right here." He squints, pointing to the building that his balcony overlooks. "There are thirty-seven windows."

"And is this how you spent your time while I was gone?"

Thunk.

The ball comes flying back at Jackson, and I move to intercept it.

"You know, you could play defense with quick reflexes like that." Jackson's approving grin does funny things to my insides. But I ignore them. Just like I always have.

"And I think someone is going a little stir-crazy."

"Of course I am!" He shoves a hand through his hair. "I don't think I've had to sit still this long since I was a kid."

I fight the laugh that threatens to burst free. Jackson looks so dejected, sitting on the couch with his leg propped up on a pillow. For as long as I've known him, Jackson has always been on the move, always having to do something. He was never one to sit idle. The frustration billowing off him is palpable.

I sit on the coffee table opposite him. Being this close to him is dangerous. I've built a neat box that I've kept "Jackson, my best friend," in over the years. But this vulnerable Jackson has the lid creaking open.

Breathing in his scent. Seeing the infinitesimal specks of gold in his eyes. The silky locks of his hair falling into his eyes. I don't want to notice these things about Jackson. I *can't* notice these things about Jackson.

Because I'm his friend. That's all I'll ever be. Lines are getting blurred because I'm staying with him. That's it.

Pushing aside the dangerous thoughts, I steer myself back to safe territory. "What can I do to help take your mind off counting windows?"

"Fuck if I know." Jackson blows out a breath, dropping his head back onto the couch. "I've already done all my exercises for the day. I'm not supposed to walk on it unless I have to. I'm useless."

"You're healing. Better to stay like this than do anything to jeopardize your knee further." I glance around the room, trying to find something we can do. It's easier to keep kindergartners occupied than a full grown man.

"The only thing in here is my old PlayStation, and I doubt you'd want to play with that," he grumbles.

"Whoa." I sit back, faking offense at his tone. "You don't think I could take you?"

Jackson's eyes rove over me. "No offense, Tenley, but you suck at video games."

I fix my gaze on him, not moving my eyes from his. "Do you see anything else you can do right now?" I quirk a brow at him, crossing my arms over my chest.

"Ugh. Fine. But I won't feel sorry when I kick your ass."

Standing, I pat Jackson on the shoulder. "We'll see about that. What game do you want to play?"

"Grab the jet ski one. I can teach you that one."

"Who says I need a lesson?" I set the disc in the tray and hand Jackson his remote.

He barks out a laugh. Jackson's never been the most open with people, but he's always been that way with me. Being in the public eye, people are always clamoring for his attention. You never know what's real and what's fake. I've seen Jackson shut himself down over the years, grumpiness coming a little easier now than it used to. But when he laughs like that? It makes my insides light up.

"The teacher thinks she knows everything, huh?" He bumps my shoulder with his as I take my spot next to him.

"I'm not as terrible as you think I am."

Jackson readies the game as we each pick our players. I settle into the armrest, putting enough distance between us that I don't have Jackson's scent overwhelming me.

Because that's what being around him is like. Over-whelming.

It'd always been easy before because I'd go home, and

he'd go home to Rachel. But now, we're stuck with each other while he's immobile. I can't remember the last time we spent this much time together.

It's breaking down the carefully constructed defenses that I put up to keep Jackson out. It was necessary, vital even, to keep my heart in one piece.

"Earth to Tenley. Have you always been this spacey?" Jackson snaps a finger in front of my face, pulling me out of my spiraling thoughts.

"Only trying to figure out a way to beat you." I try to add levity to my voice so Jackson won't pester me anymore.

"You ready?" Jackson asks.

I turn my focus to the TV, breaking eye contact. "Are you?" I steel my spine as Jackson starts the game.

"Don't worry, I'll go easy on you."

"WHERE THE FUCK did you learn to play like that?" Jackson throws his remote down in a huff.

I can't keep the cocky grin from my face as I tuck my feet under me on the couch. The sun has long since set, casting deep shadows in the living room.

"I have nephews. I've learned a thing or two over the years."

"Had I known, I would've gone a lot harder on you."

I mock a pout. "Poor you and not winning. Blow to your ego?"

"I want a rematch," he grumbles.

I shove his shoulder. "I forgot what a sore loser you are."

"I am not!" he shouts.

I lean against the armrest, quirking a brow at him. "Oh really?"

Jackson nods his head, reminding me of my students. "It's not being a sore loser if you weren't on even ground to start with."

"Fine. I'll give you a rematch." I grab the controller and smack it down into his awaiting hand. He yanks me closer. The look in his eyes has flutters erupting in my belly.

"Want to bet on it?"

"What do you have in mind?"

"Loser has to cook dinner for the week," Jackson says with all the confidence of a man who will win.

"Is that really a fair bet when you can't even stand on your leg?"

Jackson releases his hold on me, and I return to the safety of my own cushion. "And just for that, it'll be two weeks."

Before I have a chance to grab my controller, Jackson has started the game. "Hey! You're cheating!"

"Didn't say we couldn't." Jackson's tongue is between his lips as his entire focus is on the game.

Guess we're playing dirty then. Launching myself from the couch, I stand in front of Jackson, blocking his view of the TV.

"Hey! That's not fair!"

"Didn't say we couldn't," I say, parroting his words right back to him.

A strong arm wraps around my waist, pulling me down right into Jackson's lap. "Your knee —" I'm cut off.

"Is fine," Jackson finishes, staring straight at me.

His arm hasn't moved, fingers digging into the soft skin at my waist. A flicker of something passes through Jackson's eyes. If I blinked, I would've missed it.

Was that lust?

Does Jackson have feelings for me? I couldn't snuff the thought out fast enough before it took hold. Jackson had always been a part of a couple. Jackson and Rachel. Rachel and Jackson. Where one went, the other usually followed.

But with her out of the picture, could he be developing feelings for me? All I know is Jackson has never looked at me like that. Just the thought of it has my toes curling.

"Maybe we should call it a draw." The raspiness in Jackson's voice has me pushing out of his arms. The loss of heat is immediate.

I nod. "No winner if we weren't playing fair." Smoothing a hand over my hair, I wave the other behind me. "Right. I'm going to order a pizza, and I'll let you know when it's here."

Jackson doesn't move, his eyes now focused on the controller in his hand. "Sounds good."

"Good."

And while we're at it, I'll do everything in my power to forget what it felt like to sit on Jackson's lap.

Because if I'm not careful, I'll want more.

And more is dangerous.

Chapter Eight

JACKSON

"Well, well, well. Look who it is." Alex's voice has me straightening. "Didn't think we'd see you back here this soon.

"It's been two weeks." I wipe my forehead. I got the all clear this morning from Paige to do some light reps in the weight room.

"A long two weeks. We miss you, man." Clapping me on the shoulder, Alex walks over to the weight bench. "Spot me?"

I nod, grabbing my water bottle to take a large swig. "Team looked good this weekend."

Alex waves me off. "Preseason is always easy. Shame what happened to Tampa's quarterback."

"Does it make me a terrible person if I say I'm glad it wasn't me?" I position myself at the top of the bench as Alex starts his reps. It's a brief reprieve from my own workout.

"I'm glad it wasn't me either. I've never seen an arm turn like that." He shudders.

"He's got a long road ahead of him."

Alex sets the bar on the rack and sits up. "Speaking of, how's your knee doing?"

"Getting better. Even the simplest workout is enough to knock the wind out of me."

Alex laughs. "It's how I feel every time I get sacked. Sucks, doesn't it?"

This is the one thing I love about Denver. The team is a family. There's no ego, and no one thinks they are better than anyone else. Five years ago, Alex Young and I started at the same time. We roomed together during our first training camp, and he's been one of my closest friends ever since.

"Rachel's taking care of you okay?" Disdain drips from his words. He's never been her biggest fan.

"We broke up."

"For now." He rolls his eyes at me.

"For good this time."

He settles back down on the bench ready to start on a new set. "Sorry if I don't believe you. I've seen it all before."

"She couldn't handle all of this. Helping me when I couldn't walk. Rehab. So I broke up with her."

"You for real?" Alex presses the bar up.

"For real. Tenley's been staying with me."

"And how's that been going?"

"It's been…fine."

Alex scoffs, finishing his set. "Bullshit. How's it actually going?"

Walking over to the floor mat, I sit my ass down and start stretching my leg. No point in doing all of this work if I'm going to injure it again. "It's weird. She's always been around, but something happened the other day."

Alex waves his hand, indicating for me to continue.

"Since when did you become such a gossip?"

"Since you dumped Rachel and now could have a nice girl for once."

"Did no one like Rachel?" Tension coils inside my head.

"It was easy to tell you weren't happy. I've never met a grumpier son of a bitch."

"Gee, thanks."

He holds his hands up in defeat. "I'm serious. I thought you'd be a bear with your knee and what not, but you're not. It's surprising. And I'm only guessing it's because of Tenley."

I couldn't hide the smile if I tried. Just thinking about playing video games with her the other day has me feeling things I've never felt toward her before.

"See? That right there." Alex points at me. "You're smiling like a fool. So what happened the other day?"

"We were playing video games and we just kind of had a moment."

"Stop the presses. You had a moment," he jests.

"I'm being serious." I scrub a hand through my growing beard. "All of a sudden I was looking at her like she wasn't Tenley. But a woman. And a fucking gorgeous one at that. You know what I mean?"

Alex goes quiet. It's not unlike him, but the sharp turn in his gaze has me ready to question him. A chance I don't get. "What are you going to do about it then?"

"Fuck if I know."

Tenley's my best friend. Would I even want to do something? Does she feel the same way? Based on the way she was looking at me the other day, it felt like it. I just don't know if that's a risk I want to take.

"Listen. It's hard stepping outside your comfort zone. I should know. But what if you're missing out on something great because you're scared?"

"Look at the captain coming in with the good advice." I laugh to hide my own nerves.

"Just sayin'. Now you going to help me finish up, or are you done?"

I shake my head. "Nah. I'm done for the day. Don't want to overdo it. I need to ice my knee before I head out."

"Can I offer you another piece of advice?" Alex stands, helping me up from my spot on the ground.

"Maybe."

"Shave that shit off your face. You look like a Yeti."

I shove him back as I leave. "Fucker."

But it feels good to be back in here. To be with my teammates. It makes me realize how much I miss this. I love the game, don't get me wrong. But being with the guys has always been the best part. Even though I'm on the sideline, it's nice to know I haven't been completely cast aside.

It adds a little extra pep in my step as I head back to my place, knowing Tenley will be there. I've never wanted to hurry back home after a workout like I do now.

That should give me the first clue about my feelings for her, but everything is so tied up in my head right now, I should wait until I'm back on the field. Maybe that'll provide the clarity I need.

That's a problem for another day. For future Jackson to worry about.

Chapter Nine

JACKSON

"**F**uck."

The razor falls from my hand as an ache shoots down my leg. I'd be worried if Paige hadn't told me this is normal during the strengthening process.

"What are you doing?"

Tenley appears in the door of my bathroom.

I hang my head, breathing through the throb in my leg. "What does it look like?"

Crossing her arms, she pins me with a stare. The teacher look, as I call it. But instead of having me shrinking away from her, it makes me want to fight. "I was told I look like a Yeti, so I figured I should shave. But I can't fucking do it. It's not like I broke my arms."

I stab a frustrated hand through my hair. I hate feeling useless.

"Sit." Tenley moves beside me.

I plop down on the side of the bathtub, feeling the relief in my knee immediately. "I hate this," I whisper, dropping my head back against the shower stall.

Tenley doesn't answer me. I peek one eye open as she

slathers cool cream on my face. "It's okay to ask for help, Jackson."

"It's all I've been doing though. I hate that I have to rely on you for everything." I blow out a breath. I was fine this afternoon working out with Alex. But now, the dull throb in my leg is just a reminder of how far I still have to go. And how I can't do the simplest thing on my own.

"I wouldn't be here if I didn't want to help." Her breath is warm against my skin as she slides the razor up my cheek. "You're lucky I'm used to dealing with stubborn people."

I close my eyes as I listen to her move. It's hypnotic. The swish of the water. The glide of the razor across my face. Tenley's bare leg brushes against mine. My fingers have a mind of their own, drifting along the smooth skin of her thigh.

"Face me." I open my eyes, turning to look at her. Her face, always so open, is drawn tight. As if she's fighting something. I tug her closer, not letting go.

Her skin is warm, so warm that it shoots through me from the slightest touch. The tips of her fingers are gentle against my face. It's the softest touch. But it has me shifting ever so slightly to hide the growing problem in my shorts.

What the actual fuck? This has never happened to me before.

It's Tenley.

All these moments are adding up. We've always been like this, so why now?

My fingers drift higher, brushing the edge of her shorts. I don't miss the breath that escapes her.

It sends my thoughts running. What would it be like if I leaned up to kiss her? If I pulled her down into my lap so she could feel what she's doing to me?

Her lips have to be as soft as they look. What sounds

would she make when I kiss her? Fuck, I bet she tastes delicious too.

"All done." Her whispered words put an end to my erratic thoughts.

"How do I look?" I flash her my best smile from where I'm sitting.

"Like my Jackson." She takes care when wiping my face off, a small smile on her own face. "Handsome as ever."

"All thanks to you." I squeeze her leg, sending her flying back and out of my hold.

"Dinner will be ready soon. That's why I came in here."

"Okay."

"Right." Tenley backs out of the bathroom, running into the door. "Dinner. Kitchen. Meet me out there."

I want to laugh at how awkward she's being, but all it does is confirm what I'm feeling. And what I now know she's feeling for me.

Maybe this could be more.

But how the fuck do we get there?

Tenley

"ARE you sure you know what you're doing?"

I huff out a breath as more water bubbles over the pot. "Yes, Jackson. I have cooked before."

But the smell in the kitchen says otherwise. I've been a frazzled mess since I walked in on Jackson trying to shave. The feel of his hand on my leg will forever be tattooed there, along with the brush of his fingertips against the hem of my shorts.

It took everything I had not to jump him right then and there. Jackson is vulnerable. He's healing. The last thing he needs to think about is jumping into a relationship.

"Do you want help?"

I spin on my heel, pointing the slotted spoon at him. "No. You don't need to be putting any weight on that knee."

He throws his hands up in defeat. "Just offering. But you might want to—"

A glob of sauce pops, sending marinara all over me and the counter. Jackson stifles a laugh as I slam the lid back on the pot.

"This is your fault."

"How is it my fault?" Jackson tears off a piece of bread and throws it in his mouth. At least that didn't burn while I helped him shave.

"Because you don't have the proper size pots to make dinner. If I was at my house, we'd be fine."

Jackson's lips tilt up at me. I hate that it makes my heart skip a beat. He doesn't give smiles easily, and when he aims one in my direction, I melt faster than butter on an August sidewalk.

I turn back to the stove, hoping the heat will hide the flush in my cheeks. I'm a mess right now, and not just from dinner. My feelings for Jackson are a pressure cooker with the heat being turned up every day. I don't know how much longer I'm going to be able to take it before I explode.

And the way Jackson was looking at me in the bathroom? It'd be enough to make a nun consider sinning.

Turning off the stove, I drain the spaghetti and plate our meals.

"Is it going to be burned?" Jackson eyes his plate with suspicion.

I smack him on his perfectly toned pec. "No! It's just the stove. If you don't want it, you can order something yourself."

Jackson shoves a forkful in his mouth. I can't help but watch as his jaw works.

"Oh shit, that's good." Jackson moans, his eyes closed.

It does dirty things to my mind that I should definitely not be thinking about.

"See?" My voice is steadier than I thought it would be. "I told you I know how to cook."

"I thought you always hated doing it in high school."

I twirl the spaghetti around my fork, taking a daintier bite than he did. "It's because my mom made me do it at least once a week and my sisters didn't have to."

Jackson snorts a laugh. "I totally forgot about that. Why didn't she make them do it?"

I roll my eyes. "Because Penny was always over at her friends' house. And you couldn't pull Nora away from her boyfriend. I guess she assumed they were being fed and was afraid I would starve when I went to college."

Jackson drops his fork and turns to me, resting his arm on the back of my chair. The heat from his arm burns into me. It's the smallest touch, but I feel it everywhere.

"Do you remember that time I came to visit you during my bye week sophomore year?"

"How could I forget?"

A hard look washes over Jackson's face. "What was that dick's name?"

"Not everyone I dated was a dick, Jackson," I admonish.

His eyes are steel. "We went to that party, and he was there making out with some other chick."

"Okay, maybe he was a dick," I whisper.

"And you got so drunk you hurled all over me."

"Can we not talk about that while eating?" I flinch at the memory. That night was hazy at best. "Between Brad and Mike, you hated any guy I dated."

His hand drifts over my shoulder, squeezing. "That's because they didn't deserve you. You were too good for them."

But I wasn't good enough for you, I want to say.

"Not all of them were bad."

"Name one." Jackson looks like he's ready to fight.

"Dylan."

We dated my senior year of college before he moved to the East Coast. He was sweet, if not a bit timid.

Jackson snorts. "The kid was so nervous, any time you looked at him, he about wet himself."

"He was sweet."

"Doesn't mean he deserved you," Jackson grumbles.

"Since you seem to be the master on who deserves me, who should I date then?" I quirk a brow at him. "Got anyone?"

His eyes turn to saucers as he stares back at me. "How did this turn into me setting you up?"

"You think I don't date the right people, so why don't you set me up with one of your teammates?" I turn in my chair, knocking his arm off the back of my seat.

"Fuck no."

"Real mature, Jackson." I cross my arms, glaring at him. "There's not one teammate of yours that would deserve me?"

"Guys can be dicks when talking about girls to other guys. That should come as no surprise to you."

If only.

"Moving on from the topic of my past boyfriends, how was therapy today?"

"I can start walking without my crutches." He pumps a fist in the air with almost no excitement.

"Jackson, stop it. That's great."

"I can do light reps and walk. A toddler can do more."

I roll my eyes. "Tomorrow, I'm taking you to City Park and we'll go for a walk. It'll be good to get out."

"You're the best, Tenley."

"And don't you forget it."

Chapter Ten

JACKSON

"Are you ready?" Tenley looks delicious in her tight running shorts and Mountain Lions tank.

If I get to watch your ass, then yes. But I don't tell her that.

"Let's get going. I'd hate to walk a one-hour mile."

She smacks me on the arm. "Stop it. We're taking it easy. I'm not letting you hurt yourself."

Summer is starting to give way to fall. It's my favorite time in Denver. The afternoons are hot, but with a cool breeze from the mountains, it's perfect.

"Are you getting excited for the first day of school?"

Tenley turns a smile on me. It's brighter than the sun in the sky. "I can't wait. It's my favorite time of year."

"You're the only person I know who loved the first day of school."

Tenley links her arm with mine as we amble down the path near the zoo. "New school supplies. First day of school outfit. I loved it all. The promise of a fresh start."

"My eternal optimist. Always seeing the good in people."

She swats at my arm. "You say that like it's a bad thing."

"I didn't mean it that way, I swear. I wish I could be more like you."

"Really?" Tenley pulls back. Her eyes are hidden behind dark sunglasses.

"Being in the spotlight makes you jaded. And I'm not even in a prime position. I can't imagine the pressure Young is under all the time."

"I experience enough of the league vicariously through you. I couldn't handle being in it myself."

I steer us around a couple pushing a stroller. "You could do it. You handle five-year-olds like a boss. Professional athletes would be no match for you."

"I'd have you all under my spell." She laughs.

That's one way to put it.

The park gets busier the deeper inside we go. The flowers from the botanical gardens waft through the park. Lavender and something else perfume the air. It reminds me of Tenley as she tells me about all of her favorite parts of being a teacher.

I could listen to her voice for hours. I never realized how soothing it is.

"Can we sit?" I stop her as we approach a cluster of trees.

"Oh no!" She gasps, dropping her eyes to my knee. "Are you feeling okay?"

"I'm fine. Just want a bit of a break."

"Okay." Finding a spot in the shade, we sit side by side. Our legs touch, sending sparks racing through me.

It's getting harder and harder to be around this woman and not acknowledge how I'm feeling.

I was blind before. Now that Rachel is gone, it's like

I'm giving myself permission to try and determine what these feelings for Tenley mean.

Her face is turned toward the sun. Freckles dot her face, and her lips turn up in a happy smile. Tiny tendrils of blonde hair stick to her face.

"How are you feeling with the season starting soon?" She breaks the silence.

I pick at clumps of grass around my knee. "I've been doing good ignoring that it's coming up."

"Hopefully you'll only be out another few weeks, and then you'll go out there and kick butt."

Laughter escapes my lips. I love that she never cusses. One of those endearing qualities of hers that I'll never tire of.

"Everything's on schedule. As long as I don't do anything stupid, I'm hoping I'll be cleared after the bye week."

"Did the doctors say that?" She pops up, latching onto my arm.

I nod.

"Jackson! Why didn't you tell me?"

"I just don't want to get my hopes up, and I know how you are."

"This is a good thing. If the doctors are happy with your progress, you're doing something right." Dusting off her hands, she stands. "We need to celebrate. Let's grab some ice cream on our way home."

"Whatever you want, Tenley."

She drops her hands to help me up, and I reach out for her. But Tenley doesn't get a good hold and I end up pulling her down. Her chest collides with mine, just inches from me.

Every cell in my body is buzzing. Neither one of us

make a move. Her eyes are locked on mine. The air stills around us.

I'm so aware of every part of her that is touching me that I'm about to combust. I want to take her lips in mine. Cross this line that we seem to have drawn for ourselves.

Tenley's eyes drift down to my lips. When I think she's going to lean in, a shout bursts through our bubble.

Fuck.

Fuck.

Fuck.

Fuck.

We were so close. Tenley pushes off of me. "You ready to go?"

I want to say no. I want to pull her back into my arms and kiss her, but the moment is gone. Shifting my weight so I can stand on my good leg, I plaster a fake-as-fuck smile on my face.

"As I'll ever be."

Chapter Eleven

JACKSON

The walk home is quiet. I can tell Tenley is swept up in her thoughts as she eats her ice cream. But it does nothing to quell this desire I have for her. For the first time in my entire life, every cell is aware of every minute move Tenley makes.

She's always been Tenley—my best friend. But now my body is taking notice. And this is a dangerous line to be walking.

When the elevator door dings on our floor, I let Tenley off first. Her abrupt halt has me crashing into her. My eyes follow hers, and it takes everything I have not to snap.

"Rachel. What are you doing here?"

Any happiness from earlier in the day is replaced with a building tension. I walk past her and open the door into my apartment. "To see you, silly."

My eyes find Tenley's as Rachel strolls past me without a care in the world. I'm anxious as to what she'll think of my ex suddenly showing up. "We broke up."

Pressure gathers behind my eyes. Tenley and I were

having a good day. The last thing I want is for Rachel to show up and screw everything up.

"Oh, you didn't mean that. You were just torn up about your knee."

"Rachel. You left me high and dry when I needed you. Why the fuck would you think I didn't mean it?" I pinch the bridge of my nose, willing myself to have patience.

"Like we haven't broken up and gotten back together before." She turns, her dark eyes settling on Tenley. "What's she doing here?"

"*She* has been here to help me. Watch your tone."

Rachel sidles up to me, running her fingers down my chest. There's no reaction. No sudden desire to take her into my arms and rekindle what we once had. I breathe a sigh of relief, knowing, for once, that I made the right decision.

"Rachel. Please. I don't want to ask you again. Leave."

The anger building in her eyes is plain as day. "You want to be with her over me?" She points behind her. "What, you're going to play seven minutes in heaven with her again and then just go back to football?"

"What in the world are you talking about?"

A squeak leaves Tenley, and my gaze shifts to hers. Her blue eyes are wide with terror at Rachel's words.

"Why would I tell you? You've made it pretty clear you don't need me."

A twinge in my knee tells me I've been standing for too long. I reach for the wall behind me, and Tenley notices immediately.

"Is your leg okay?" Her voice is quiet, like she doesn't want to draw any more attention to herself than she already has.

"So cute. She finally thinks she has a chance with you." Rachel's words are bitter. She eyes her up and down, like a lioness going in for the kill. "Better you than me. He's a terrible lay, and all he cares about is football."

And with her parting words, she slams the door behind her.

Scrubbing a hand down my face, I turn to face Tenley as best I can. "What in the world was she talking about?"

"Why would I have any idea?" Tenley turns her back on me, walking into the kitchen. Now I know she's lying to me.

She's messing around with the dirty dishes in the sink. "Tenley." My voice is firm, trying to bring her attention to me.

Plates clatter down in the sink as she turns to face me, her hands clutching the counter with more force than necessary.

"There's nothing to talk about." Tenley's words are quiet as I walk over to her.

"Tell me."

When she turns around, her eyes are wet. I want to pull her into my arms if Rachel caused her any hurt. I'd burn down the entire world if it meant keeping her safe.

Tenley starts picking at her fingernail, not looking at me. It's making me more nervous, then she finally opens her mouth.

"It was me."

"What was?"

She blows out a breath. "At that party in high school. It was me in the closet."

I shake my head, not understanding her. "No it wasn't. You weren't there."

"Glad I was so forgettable." She rolls her eyes at me, sarcasm dripping from every word. "I left early because I missed my curfew."

"I would've known if you were there." It's not sinking in.

"I went with Gabby. We were late, and they were just getting started playing the game. You were talking to Rachel at the time."

Fucking Rachel. "Why didn't you say hi when you were there?"

A sardonic laugh bubbles out of her. It's not something I'm used to. "I had a major crush on you in high school. It was hard talking to you when you were around other girls."

"Had?" I hate that I'm disappointed at hearing this. Tenley has always been in my life. She always will be in my life. But something's shifted lately. I don't know if it's that I'm relying on her more than usual, but the things I'm feeling for her are new. And I want her to reciprocate.

But when Tenley looks at me, her face is shocked. I move onto the stool, unable to hold myself up anymore. "Had a crush, Tenley?"

"We really don't need to be talking about this."

"Yes we do!" I snap. My patience is gone tonight with anyone of the opposite sex. First with the woman who rolled back in here thinking she was entitled to me, and now with the woman standing in front of me not telling me anything.

"Fine!" Except when Tenley snaps, I sit up and take notice. "It was me you kissed that night. We weren't supposed to talk, but you tripped when you came in and I knew it was you immediately. Then you said, 'you're a really good kisser.' I couldn't wait to tell you, but then I got the text from my mom and had to leave, and by the time I got to school on Monday, you were with Rachel."

The speed at which she fires that off has my head spinning. "But why would Rachel say it was her?"

"Because everyone had a crush on you in high school!

You were the new football player and everyone wanted your attention. God, sometimes you're so thick, it astounds me."

"Well, sorry if I'm not processing this as quickly as you. I only just found out that the best kiss of my life was with my best friend and not my girlfriend of the last thirteen years. Why didn't you say anything?"

Tenley crosses her arms, piercing me with a fierce look. "Because you were dating Rachel. I wasn't going to come between you two. Besides, Rachel is scary on a good day."

I huff out a laugh. "You're not wrong."

"Listen, I know you need help, but I can't be here right now."

"What? Why?" I don't want Tenley to leave. The tenuous grip I have on my sanity is close to snapping. Again.

"Because I need time to cool off."

"Why are you always so levelheaded?" I mutter.

"I'm a kindergarten teacher. I have to be." Tenley walks over to the entry table and grabs her purse and keys. "Look, I'll be back later, but just…don't do anything to hurt yourself, or I'd never forgive myself, okay?"

I nod at her as she turns to leave.

Fuck.

In the matter of an hour, my entire world has shifted. What I thought was written in stone was shattered. It's become dust, blown out by the truth that Tenley laid bare for me.

The best kiss of my life—the one that led me to Rachel, to stay with her through high school, college, hell, even the draft and my first few years in the NFL—was Tenley.

My best friend.

The one who dropped everything to help me in my time of need.

Tenley, who has always been there for me. She was there at my first college game, even though we didn't go to the same school. She was there for me in the hospital when my appendix burst our senior year and I missed homecoming.

It was always her. Never Rachel in those memories, but Tenley.

What would have happened if she'd never left that party? Would we be together now?

These last few weeks spin through my head. Every move. Every touch.

Has Tenley always felt this way? I mean, I would know if she did, right?

I'm seeing my Tenley through a different filter now.

My Tenley.

She's never been mine in that sense, but even then, that's how I've always thought of her. Could I actually have her now? Does she still want me? Would we even work well as a couple?

My mind is spinning as I drift off to sleep. But one thing is apparent now.

It's Tenley.

And I want to make her mine.

Chapter Twelve

TENLEY

"Holy shit! Are you serious?"

I nod, knocking back the rest of the wine in my glass. As soon as I left Jackson's, I went straight to Gabby's. As much as I love my sisters, this called for my best friend. "Rachel just blew everything wide open. Jackson looked at me like he had no idea who I was."

"And now he knows that it was you that night?"

"Yup." I pop the p, pouring more wine into my glass.

"I wish I wasn't breastfeeding in an hour and could drink with you." She looks longingly at the bottle. "So what are you going to do?"

"I've wanted Jackson my entire life," I say, my voice small. "What if we finally get this chance and it doesn't work? I can't lose him."

Gabby grasps my arm. "Why do you think you'll lose him? What if this is finally your time?"

"Not all of us get lucky enough to marry our high school sweetheart."

Gabby rolls her eyes at me. "I'm not talking marriage.

Maybe instead of hanging out with me, you go back and hang out with him."

I gulp my wine. "I'm nervous." I hate admitting it, but I am. "He looked totally freaked-out."

The smile she gives me is conniving. "Yeah, because you rocked his world."

"Well, as much as one's world can be rocked by a single conversation."

"Please. If that kiss means half as much to him as it does to you, I think this could be the beginning of something good." Gabby laughs.

"What's so funny?"

"Can you imagine what a good kisser he is now? I bet he knows his way around a set of lips now."

I snort, almost spewing my sip of wine all over the coffee table. "Gabby! You cannot say things like that."

"As your best friend, it's my prerogative to make sure you don't end up with someone I don't like. And I like Jackson. That man will most certainly know how to please you in bed."

"Stop." I cover my ears, not believing what I'm hearing. "You jumped from kissing to orgasms so fast, I can't handle it."

Gabby pulls my hand down. "Oh, stop it. As much as I want you to rush back to his place tonight, you've had too much wine. You're going to crash here, and then tomorrow, you are going to tell me all about what happens."

A crying baby signals Gabby's departure.

Sinking into the couch, I squelch the feelings swirling inside of me.

I got scared and ran. I didn't want to stick around to see if Jackson would turn me down. But at the same time, could this be the start of everything I've always wanted?

DEEP BREATHS, *Tenley. Deep breaths.*

I've been standing outside Jackson's apartment door for the better part of ten minutes. I know he spent the day at the team facility working out, while I got the last few things wrapped up at school before the first day next week.

It took all day for me to get even the most basic things done. My mind was never far from Jackson. I can't hide from him forever, no matter how much I want to.

Steeling my nerves, I push my key into the lock and open the door to Jackson's apartment. I can't remember the last time I was so nervous to walk into his place. Maybe I'll get lucky and he'll still be out.

"Tenley? Is that you?"

I wasn't that lucky. Dropping my bag, I find him sitting in the living room with the lights low. The Denver skyline casts him in an ethereal glow.

"It's me." I toe off my shoes and walk over to him. Butterflies threaten to explode out of me. I've never been nervous around Jackson, and I hate it.

"For a second there, I didn't think you'd be coming back."

The smile I give him is strained. "A lot happened yesterday, and it kind of through me for a loop."

Jackson stands, scrubbing a hand through the stubble lining his jaw. "Why didn't you ever tell me?"

His voice is calm.

I look down at my toes curling in the shag of the rug on the floor. "Because you were dating Rachel, like I said. And I never thought it was my place."

Jackson's dark eyes rake over me. It's a slow caress,

goose bumps rippling out with each sweep of his eyes. I've never felt more exposed to Jackson than I do right now.

Every feeling, every moment, is wide open for his perusal.

"Dance with me, Tenley."

My eyes flick to meet his as he extends a hand to me. My voice escapes me as I take his hand in mine, callouses from years of football greet my smooth palm. Linking our hands, Jackson pulls me close to him, our hands resting on his chest. My heart is aching after my confession. After yelling at him that it was me in that closet in high school.

His muscles flex under my fingers as I bury my face in his chest. Bringing our joined hands to cover his heart, he spins us, my head swirling.

Where was my grump of a best friend? The one who made me laugh when my grandma died by sticking fries up his nose? Who always let me steal sips of his Coke?

Every voice that ever told me Jackson would never notice me is quiet as he holds me in his arms. I've never been held like this. Like I'm cared for and protected and safe. I never want to leave the bubble of Jackson's arms. It's like they were made just for me.

Jackson stops, pulling back a bit. The lights reflect in his deep brown eyes. They shimmer with something I don't want to put a name to. His large hand cups my cheek, causing my heart to fly to my throat. I hold my breath, waiting to see what he'll do.

Softly, oh so softly, Jackson presses his lips to mine. My body is set on fire at the merest of touches. And as quickly as it starts, it's over. As if it were a dream.

I want to cry out and pull him back. Tell him that it wasn't enough. That I need his kisses as much as the air I breathe.

But then they're back, firm and commanding.

I can't help the way my body arches into him, wanting to close the distance. To feel the hard planes of his chest against me. I drink in the kiss as he parts my lips.

He's familiar and new. Home and uncharted lands. I want to explore every inch of his mouth.

We've stopped moving, standing in the waning light of his living room. My hands try to find purchase on him. His hands drift down my sides, cradling my hips. When his tongue touches mine, he swallows my gasp. It's better than I remember. Every kiss has been compared to Jackson in that closet in ninth grade.

And no one has ever lived up to it.

But this Jackson? This Jackson is all man. He knows how to kiss and set me on fire with the slightest of touches. I don't know if I'll ever recover from this kiss.

Jackson pulls back, dropping his forehead against my own. I fist my hands in his shirt, wanting to keep him near.

"Jackson."

"I know, Tenley. I know."

His thumb brushes against my swollen lips. The air is electric around us, pulsing, beating, lighting the passion that's coming off us in waves.

This kiss has split me wide open. My heart is Jackson's for the taking, and I can only hope he guards it with his life.

Chapter Thirteen

JACKSON

"You must have the football gods on your side, because your knee is looking great," the doctor says while examining my latest scans.

"I've been doing exactly as you said, taking it easy and only doing the exercises Paige has given me."

He laughs. "She scares me, so it's a good thing you're listening. I'll let her know we can increase your training."

"No chance in coming back any sooner?" I ask, hope coating my voice.

"No chance. I don't want you overdoing it and then not being able to come back at all this season."

I shove a frustrated hand through my hair. "I know. Just want to be back on the field with the guys."

"You'll get there. Don't worry."

"Thanks, doc."

Pushing off the exam table, I head back to the weight room. A few guys still linger after morning workouts.

"Fields."

"Fisher." I nod to Knox as he works through a set on a weight machine.

"How's the knee?"

I find a weight machine near him to work my upper body. "On the right path. Hopefully I'll be back before the bye week."

"Damn. That's awesome. Rookie is good, but we need you."

"I can't believe this will be the first season opener I've missed."

"You're lucky there's not as much competition for your position." Knox's face hardens. No player ever wants to think about someone else taking their position on the field.

"You two ladies done chatting in here?"

Knox winces at the voice immediately.

Frankie, the linebacker coach, walks into the weight room. Her no-fucks-given attitude is strong today.

"Is it a crime to check on a fellow captain to see how he's doing?" His face is hard as he takes her in, but she isn't swayed.

"And as a captain, I need you out on the field so we can run drills."

"Fucking hard-ass," he whispers.

"Sorry, what was that?" Frankie turns an ear to him. "Couldn't quite hear you. I think what you meant to say was 'yes, coach.'"

My eyes volley back and forth between the two.

"Field. Now, Fisher." She storms off.

"Shit. I'm glad she's not my coach."

Knox grumbles. "I have no idea what I did to piss her off, but I know I'm going to pay for it later."

"Better you than me."

Knox gives me a wary look. "I gotta get out there. You still coming out with the boys this afternoon?"

I nod. "It's tradition, and we can't fuck with tradition."

"Damn straight." Knox holds his fist out, and I bump

mine against his. "Don't overdo it. I want you back out there."

"You and me both, man."

"WHO'S BUYING THE NEXT ROUND?" Knox slams down his drink as he looks around our tiny booth. It'd be fine for regular size people, but cram in five athletes and we overwhelm the space.

"I bought the first round, so not me." Alex pushes back in his seat, looking around the quiet bar. I don't know how he found this place, but we can be ignored here.

Football players at a books and wine bar? No one would ever believe it.

"Credit card roulette?" Colin asks, sipping on his own cocktail.

I throw my card down. "I'm in."

"I hate you guys," Alex bemoans as he takes out his own card.

A sneaky smile crosses his face as we each lay down our cards. Our waiter walks by, and not being the first time we've been here, he starts grabbing cards until only one is left.

"Are you fucking kidding me? I've bought three times in a row! Why can't the rookie pay?" Alex gripes.

"Sorry, QB. I don't make the big bucks like you," Logan pokes at him, Alex's fake annoyance growing.

"Careful, Logan." Alex laughs. "You might miss out on some plays because of it."

"Ohh, I'd love to tackle our newest running back." Knox rubs his hands together as our waiter comes back with another round of drinks.

Logan visibly flinches away from Knox. As one of our bigger linebackers, he's a force to be reckoned with.

"As long as someone gets one on Allen, I'm good." I sip my whiskey, leaning back in my seat.

"Is that the guy who hit you?" Logan asks.

I nod, slicking my tongue across my lips. I'm still bitter that he knocked me out.

"He's a dirty player. Always out to hurt someone, so always keep your eyes peeled for him." I direct my comment to Logan.

"I played with him in college, and he was dirty back then," Alex states.

"Is this what you guys do? Sit around gossiping about other players before the season starts?" Logan's eyes dart around the small booth.

"Nah, something we started doing after we all roomed together during training camp," I say. "Coach wanted all the lines to bond, so he roomed different positions together."

"And we all kind of stuck together after that," Knox chimes in. "These fuckers can't get enough of my handsome face."

"Speak for yourself," Alex laughs over his drink.

"We started doing it before the season starts after our last preseason game. Way to chill out and relax before the craziness of the season starts," I tell Logan as the other guys start talking about plays on the offense.

It's one of the things I love most about football. Not just the sport, but the camaraderie.

I've been playing with these guys, rookie notwithstanding, for the last five years. We've become a family. Some players, some teams, are only out for themselves. But not Denver.

From day one, it's been a family environment.

Everyone plays for the good of the team. If one person is hurting, we're all hurting. It's next man up so we're always there for one another.

"How's the knee feeling, Fields?" Alex interrupts.

"It finally feels like it's not in a vise. Thank God. But don't tell Paige that. I don't want her coming at me with harder exercises. It wouldn't surprise me if she was a drill sergeant in a past life."

Alex laughs. We've all been there with her.

"I don't know how you managed to stay off your feet for that long. I'd go crazy." Colin slaps my shoulder from beside me.

I hide my smile behind my glass. "It wasn't that bad."

"Wasn't that bad? What's that face for?" Colin quirks a brow at me.

"Nothing. I'm just saying it could've been worse. I could've torn my ACL and then been shit out of luck."

"Nope. I know that look. There's a girl." Knox slaps a hand on the table, almost knocking the drinks over on the wobbly table.

"I thought Rachel wasn't around."

"Who's Rachel?" Logan asks.

"Ahh, rookie. You have so much to learn." Colin gives him one of his press-ready smiles.

"If it's not Rachel, then who is it?"

"You guys are worse than my sister and her friends."

Alex only shrugs his shoulder. "What can we say? It means we care."

I blow out a breath I didn't realize I was holding. "There's someone."

"Do we need more drinks for this?" Knox downs the rest of his drink and signals to our waiter for another round.

"I'm good." I wave, sipping on my still-full drink.

"So who's the new chick?" Logan asks.

"Careful, Winchester." It takes everything I have not to grind my teeth at how he refers to Tenley.

"Wow. So who is this woman?" Alex asks, leaning back into the booth.

A smile hits me as I think about Tenley. "I've known Tenley since my family moved to Denver when I was in high school."

"And you never dated her?" Logan asks.

I shake my head. "I started dating Rachel, and it took me a while to realize she wasn't the one for me."

"A while? A while is my grandma trying to teach my mom how to cook." Knox rolls his eyes. "You've been dating her for almost thirteen years!"

I reach across the table and smack him. "Dated being the key word now."

"So how serious is this?" Alex pipes up.

It's the thing I've always liked about Alex. He's always been one of the steadiest guys on the team. Doesn't raise his voice and is always there for anyone who needs him.

But he's also asking me the question I don't know the answer to. We just kissed last night before we were each pulled away. With school starting for her and my rehab ramping up, our time together will be more limited.

I know we'll need to have a conversation soon. With the season starting soon and trying to get my knee back to where it was before, starting a relationship should be the last thing on my mind.

But it's Tenley.

"It's still new," I settle on.

All I wanted to do today was get back to her. This is nothing like it was with Rachel. Every time I think about it, I want to smack myself in the head for being so dense.

Every soft look from her, every smile, every laugh

makes me want to fall to my knees in front of her and worship her. Just to see her look at me like that.

"Shit. You're in deep already," Alex whispers so only I can hear.

I straighten, adjusting my leg under the table.

"No I'm not." My tone is too defensive. "I have football to focus on right now. Getting back to the game."

Alex takes the hint, steering the conversation away from the heavy stuff. "As long as you keep rehabbing, you'll be back before you know it."

I down the rest of my drink, feeling the burn in my chest. "I hate that I can't be out there with you guys. It kills me."

"You take care of your knee. And maybe hook a guy up if Tenley has a sister?" Logan wiggles his eyebrows at me.

"God, you guys are terrible." I laugh. "I wouldn't let you near her with a ten-foot pole. Her sisters are not available for you."

"Thank God for that! Can you imagine having this guy as your brother-in-law?" Knox laughs.

Logan throws a handful of nuts at him.

"Watch it! If you get us banned from this place, rook, then you'll never be invited back."

His face pales at the thought. "Shit, sorry."

Knox grasps his shoulder, pinning him with a stare that would take down a lesser man. What Tenley would call his scary football face. "This place is sacred, rookie. We only bring select people here. So don't go blowing it by being a dick or inviting jersey chasers. This is our space. Got it?"

Logan swallows, nodding in response.

"Stop being a dick and scaring the kid." Alex rolls his eyes at Knox.

"Someone has to teach him." Knox shrugs his shoulders.

"In all seriousness, guys." Alex clears his throat, taking command of the space around us. "I'm hoping this is our year. We've been fighting together for longer than I care to admit with no trophy to show for it. I don't want to jinx us,"—everyone around him knocks on the wooden table and he laughs—"but this is one of the best teams we've had in years. If we keep grinding, keep digging, I know we can do it."

The tension around the table is high. Everyone wants to win the big game. We hardly talk about it, but this is the one chance we give ourselves every year, this small group of guys I've come to trust with my own life.

But a sadness also seeps in. Because for the first time, they'll be lacing up their cleats without me. I'll be on the outside looking in. And I hate it. I hate that I won't be there for my team. They said I could be back by early October, but you never know with a knee injury.

"So lean on each other. Tell me if you need help; tell Knox, any of the guys here. We're your captains, and we want to help you help us win."

Alex pins each of us with a look, letting us know he means business.

"Let's have a great season, boys. To the Mountain Lions."

We all clink our drinks in cheers, liquid spilling all over the table. "To the Mountain Lions!"

Chapter Fourteen

JACKSON

"So how was your first day at school?"

Tenley's smile hits me square in the chest. "It was just a meet-the-teacher day. We start Monday. But they are a great group. It's always hard to tell with the parents being there, but I'm so excited."

Her excitement is palpable. After I finished up with the boys, I brought dinner home for both of us because I figured she would be tired. Quite the opposite. She's vibrating with energy.

Listening to her talk is mesmerizing. Sitting at the small table on my balcony, her knees are wedged in between mine.

My focus is solely on her lips. Fuck. those lips. I'm practically obsessed with them after a few kisses.

Their softness.

Their responsiveness.

Those soft moans that escape when I'm kissing her.

The summer air is hot around us.

"Are you listening to me, Jackson?"

I shake my head, not even bothering to pretend otherwise. "Sorry. I got distracted."

"By?" She's using her teacher voice. It shouldn't be such a turn-on, but fuck me. My dick is practically drooling for her.

"Your lips."

Hooking my hands under her knees, I pull her closer to me. Close enough that I can see the visceral reaction she is having to me.

Nipples tighten under her dress. Pupils widen. Tongue darts out to wet her lips.

I take that as my cue.

Dipping my head down, I capture her lips with mine.

It's even better than I remember. I don't know how I could have confused her kisses with Rachel's. It's no contest.

I get lost in the moment, easily sinking into this kiss. Leaning back, I pull Tenley onto my lap. Her soft moan lets me know she feels how hard I am for her.

Soft fingers plays with the hair at the nape of my neck.

There's nothing hurried about this kiss. We're learning and exploring each other.

It's a new sensation, feeling these kinds of things for Tenley. She's always been in my life, but feeling her soft curves under my hands is new. I should take things slow with her, but that's about the last thing on my mind when she's taking just as much from this kiss as I am.

Like she wants me to devour her.

I run a hand up her arm, cupping her cheek and deepening the kiss.

It's like she's a magnet, drawn to me. The closer she gets, the deeper I kiss her. My hand wanders, feeling the softness of her skin under my rough hands. I slide one hand higher, lifting the hem of her dress.

God, she is so soft. I want to know what her skin tastes like.

"Jackson."

It's a plea. Standing, I take her hand in mine and lead her back to my room. I pull her back to me, wanting her in my arms. It's the only place she should ever be.

The wanton need in her eyes as I sit on the bed has me sucking in a breath to steady myself.

This is Tenley.

My best friend. The one person who has always been there for me. And crossing this line with her feels significant. Like we won't be able to come back from it.

"You okay?" Her fingers caress my cheek, bringing me back to the moment.

Leaning back, I pull her down on top of me. Blonde hair falls around our faces.

"It's just…" I let out a sigh, warring with myself if I should tell her.

"It's okay to be nervous." Her breath is warm on my lips as she tells me exactly what I'm feeling.

"I have done this before, you know," I huff out on a laugh.

"Not with me, you haven't. It's a big deal to me too."

Just knowing she feels the same way has that uneasy piece falling away, leaving only the woman lying on top of me in its wake.

"Do you know how sexy you are when you say things that make perfect sense?"

She shrugs a shoulder. "I try."

I flip us over, my lips attacking hers once again. The last kiss was soft and slow. But this one is full of need and lust. Desire to feel every part of her against every part of me.

My fingers drift under her dress, pulling it higher and

higher. A smile nearly splits my face in two at seeing all her pale skin underneath. I want to take my time with her, worship her, but I also know that if I don't get my lips on her, I might damn near come apart at the seams.

I drag my finger along the waistband of her underwear. She squirms under my touch.

"You like that?"

"Yes. God, yes." She brings my mouth back to hers. "I really like kissing you."

"What was it I told you all those years ago?" I drag my lips down her jaw, nibbling on her earlobe. "You're a really good kisser."

"Uh-huh." Tenley is writhing beneath me.

"You're a fucking phenomenal kisser now." I crush my lips back to hers, drinking her in. Every pass of her tongue against mine has my cock threatening to burst out of my pants. I've never felt like this from kissing.

I knew it then, and I know it now. Tenley is the best fucking kisser.

Sitting back, I stare down at the lust-filled face of my best friend. Grabbing the back of my shirt, I pull it off. I don't miss the way her eyes drink me in.

"It's unfair you look this good without a shirt on."

I smirk as her fingers drag over my abs.

"Like ridiculously good."

"It's a shame I'm the only one half-naked."

Settling between her legs, I push her dress up, over her head, and off to the floor. More skin is exposed. Her tits are heaving with each breath, an invitation to know them. I kiss the soft swells spilling over the cups. Her nails drag down my back as my fingers toy with the edge of her bra.

Pulling the cotton of one cup down, a dusky, tight nipple is ripe for the taking. I circle my tongue around it, keeping my eyes on Tenley's.

"Oh God, that feels good."

I smile as I take it between my teeth, my other hand drifting down her stomach to play with her panties. The way Tenley responds to me, her body arching into mine, has me thinking of game film to keep myself from coming too soon.

The slight twinge in my knee has me wincing, pulling me back to reality.

"Fuck."

"Are you okay?" Tenley's voice is soft as she pushes up on her elbows to look at me. "Is it your knee?"

"You might have to take the lead on this."

"Should we stop?" God, this woman. The care in her voice is something I've never felt before. Never have I been with someone who showed me so much care, and dare I say, love.

"Fuck, no." Taking her hand in mine, I pull her up to stand with me. Taking off the rest of my clothes, I unclasp her bra and take her in.

There is nothing that could stop me from loving this woman tonight.

"When I said you have to take the lead, I meant it."

I let my eyes drift down, noticing the goose bumps breaking out on her skin. I sink back onto the bed, maneuvering myself so I'm in the center. I feel her eyes everywhere as I give myself a lazy stroke.

Tenley shimmies out of her underwear. I'm drooling. The most beautiful woman in the world is naked in front of me and I'm about to lose my damn mind if she doesn't touch me.

Setting one knee on the bed, she slides a hand up my thigh.

"I don't know what I want to do first."

The hunger in her voice has me squeezing the base of my cock. Rachel never made me feel this alive.

I lick my lips, wanting her mouth everywhere on me.

"Get over here." My voice is harsh as I beckon her to me.

"I thought you said I was taking the lead." She crawls on all fours over to me, her lips hovering above mine. "If this is you not taking the lead, you don't follow instructions very well."

She gives me a soft kiss before pulling back.

"Ya gotta give me something, Tenley. I'm fucking dying here."

I squeeze my dick, trying to stave off the release gathering in my balls. The image of Tenley moving toward me, naked, will forever be burned into my brain.

"Let's see how good you are at following instructions."

Fuck, where did this sex goddess come from? I groan, nodding at her.

"Good. Now, hands behind your head."

I do as she says. The smile she gives me tells me she's pleased.

But I lose all thought when her hand wraps around my cock. "Fuck."

Her fingers barely touch, but the sight of her wrapped around me is sinful. This sweet girl I've known almost half my life is causing dirty things to pop up in my mind.

"See? When you're good at listening, you get rewarded."

The smile she gives me is confident right before she takes the crown of my dick into her mouth.

"Shit," I hiss out. The warmth of her mouth on me is enough to make me come. Not thinking, I run a hand through her hair.

"Uh-uh." She pulls back, her tits swaying ever so gently as she sits on her heels. "What did I say?"

"Seriously?" I growl.

She nods. "If I'm taking the lead, then you need to listen."

"Only for you, Tenley." It takes all the self-control I have to pull my hands away from her. We've barely scratched the surface of what we can do, but I'm loving this already.

"Good." And then she swallows me to the back of her throat. My hands clench in my hair to keep from touching her. I want to thrust farther into her mouth, but I don't. Because I don't want her to move.

"Fuck. If you keep doing that, I'm going to come embarrassingly fast."

She pulls off me with a pop, her lips swollen. "Well, we wouldn't want that, would we?"

Tenley drops soft kisses up my stomach, licking across each ab. She pinches my nipple as her lips find mine. She's driving me mad with need. I want to be inside her. Feel her pussy clamp down on my dick as she comes around me.

"Condom?" It's like she's reading my mind.

"Nightstand." Another kiss before she pulls back. "You have a phenomenal ass."

Tenley's blue eyes peer back over her shoulder as she shakes it at me.

Who knew under that sweet facade was a sex vixen? Someone sent to tempt me and who no doubt will give me the best fucking orgasm of my life.

My Tenley.

My sweet girl, Tenley.

Also known as sex goddess Tenley.

She turns around, opening the condom and rolling it

down my hard length. I thrust up into her hand as she moves over my lap, gliding her slick pussy over my dick.

"You're playing with fire, Tenley. If you don't start moving, I might have to take matters into my own hands."

"We wouldn't want that, now would we?" She quirks a brow right before guiding me to her entrance and sinking down. Inch by slow, painful inch.

"Oh my God." Tenley tosses her head back as her hands find purchase on my chest. This time, when I move my hands to her hips, she doesn't say a word.

I'm about ready to lose my mind at how good it feels to be inside her. At how warm and wet she is. It's like we were made for each other.

Tenley rocks her hips, moving over me. I sit up, taking one hard nipple into my mouth. Her hands hold me tight to her.

We're moving as one. The tension swirling around us is at a breaking point. I lick up the bead of sweat that settles between the valley of her breasts.

"I'm so close, Jackson." Her movements become more frenzied as I thrust up into her. My own orgasm is right there, but I'm not coming until she does.

"Come for me." I kiss a path up her chest, hot kisses on her neck before nibbling on her ear. "Come, Tenley."

All it takes is a few more thrusts and she's coming unglued. Her pussy squeezes my dick to within an inch of its life as my own orgasm bursts out of me in a rush of white-hot pleasure.

"Fuck. Fuck, fuck, fuck," I shout, holding Tenley to me as we ride the waves of our climax together.

It's intense. It's powerful. It's like nothing I've ever experienced in my life.

I collapse back against the bed, taking her with me.

Our breaths are heavy as we come down from our high. I wrap her in my arms, loving how relaxed she feels.

"That was indescribable." She turns her head, sated eyes meeting mine. I drag a finger down her back, settling my palm on her ass.

"I kind of like you taking the lead."

"I did too." She kisses just above my heart.

I give her ass a hearty squeeze, enjoying the moan that slips out. "But next time, I'm punishing you for all that teasing."

"Mmm, I can't wait."

Chapter Fifteen

JACKSON

"What are you working on?"

Tenley spins a lock of hair around her finger. She's sitting across from me on the couch. It was a long day rehabbing my knee. Paige does not take it easy on me, and while I appreciate it, I'm also tired as fuck.

"Just planning out our Friday Favorites for class."

I pinch my brows. "What's Friday Favorites?"

"I let the students talk about their favorite thing from the week. Or we do a show and tell. It changes depending on what I know has happened during the week."

"And the kids like that?"

Tenley shifts her gaze to me, nodding "They love it. They're kind of like football players. Love talking about themselves."

I want to kiss away the smirk on her face. "Oh yeah? Who says we like talking about ourselves?"

"I've seen the way some of your teammates eat up the media attention."

Grabbing her hand, I pull her down onto my lap.

"Teammates, yes. Me? I'd rather be stuck in the desert for a month."

"That's a touch dramatic." Tenley rolls her eyes at me but wraps an arm around my shoulders. Moments like this, these small moments where she's in my arms, hit me like lightning. I've been missing out on this my entire life.

I love feeling Tenley's soft curves under my hands. Having her hold me in her arms. Rachel was always so concerned about appearances that she was constantly scrolling on her phone, keeping up with the latest social media craze.

But the only time Tenley isn't here with me? She's focusing on her students. The passion she has for teaching is the same I feel for football.

I peer over her shoulder at her notes. "Football?"

She tucks the notebook away. "Why not? All the students love football in one way or another, so I figured maybe we could do a football Friday?"

"How about an appearance by your favorite player?"

Tenley looks at me with delight in her eyes. "You think Alex would be available to come this week?"

I throw her down on the couch, tickling her sides. Giggles burst out of her. "Who knew I was living with such a comedian?"

"Stop! Stop! I'm kidding." She huffs out a breath, peering up at me with her baby blues that I could get lost in. "Is Knox around? Maybe he'll come if Alex can't."

"I see where I stand then," I push back, feigning anger.

"Oh, poor baby. You don't like not being my favorite?" She snakes a finger in the V of my tee, pulling me back down to her.

Pushing out my bottom lip, I mock a pout. "I should be your only favorite."

Tenley leans up, capturing my lips with hers. I relish

her taste as her tongue dips out to tangle with mine. Pressing my weight down on her, I run a hand down her side, hiking her leg up over my hip. I could get lost in her. In the sweet smell of strawberries that has taken over my apartment. In the feel of her soft curves beneath me. The moans that escape her as my lips trail a path down her jaw.

I pull back as Tenley follows me up, trying to take me in another kiss. I smile at the whimper as it leaves her lips.

"Tell me I'm your favorite."

"You're my favorite."

I smile against her lips. "You're lying."

Tenley grasps my head in her hands, my eyes focusing on hers. "Do you think I'd be here if you weren't?"

I drop an easy kiss on her lips and pull back. "I just like giving you shit."

Fisting her hand in my shirt, Tenley pulls me back down to her. "There's not a lot of people that I'd do this for. And by a lot of people, exactly six. My family, Gabby, and you. So you should consider yourself very lucky, Mr. Fields."

I groan, my dick thickening in my pants. Those words off her lips send all blood racing south. I want to worship at her feet. Spend the night buried inside of her, showing this woman just how much she's my favorite. But instead, she's pushing herself off of me.

"I wasn't done with you," I say, trying to grab for her.

"Guess you'll just have to wait until later then."

"ARE YOU READY?" Tenley asks, dropping her hands onto my shoulders.

"Is it bad that I'm nervous?" My eyes look around the empty classroom, waiting for her class to get back from art.

Stealing a quick kiss, Tenley makes her way over to the board. "They're kindergartners. Not much to be scared of."

I run a hand through my hair. "What if they ask inappropriate questions?"

Tenley rolls her eyes at me. "The worst question they are going to ask is if your pads are smelly after a game."

Groaning, I slap a hand to my head. "I am not prepared for kids."

"You'll be fine, promise."

"And if I'm not?" I stand, making my way over to her.

She glances around, making sure the room is empty. "Then I'll make sure you're okay later."

"You're killing me, woman." The classroom door bursts open, and I jump back from her. I was at least three feet from her, but it's like when I was in high school and my dad would come into my room unannounced.

Fifteen tiny humans stare up at me as they take their seats around the ABC carpet.

"Whoa! Do you know who you are?" a kid with short brown hair asks me.

I nod, crossing my arms as I look down at him. "Yeah. Who are you?"

"Billy. How come you're not playing football?" He cocks an eyebrow at me, showing me a toothy grin.

"Alright, Billy, everyone. Take a seat. We have a special guest here today." Tenley claps her hands and everyone sits, turning to give her their full attention. I've never seen this side of Tenley.

Tenley is soft, yet powerful. The way she takes command of her classroom has me about ready to plonk down on the carpet with the rest of the kids and do whatever she says. She's not bossy, but shows every single kid respect.

"Our special guest today for Friday Favorites is my friend Mr. Jackson. Can someone tell me where you might know him from?"

A few hands, Billy's included, shoot up into the air. Tenley calls on a little girl who's bouncing up and down where she sits. "He plays for Denver!" Her voice is excited as she shouts it out to everyone.

"He does. And does anyone know what position?" Tenley turns her wide smile on me as she calls on another student.

"He kicks the points after a touchdown. My dad says we need him back."

I try not to wince at his words. "Hopefully I'll be back in a few weeks."

Tenley gives me a sweet smile before turning her attention back to her students. "Does anyone have any questions for Mr. Jackson?"

A hand shoots up into the air followed by a question. "What's it like to play football?"

This one is easy. "It's the best. I love being able to play for my hometown. The Mountain Lions are the best team out there."

A few kids do the team growl that the fans do before each game. A bone-deep ache settles inside me. It's what the guys do before we break our huddle and run out onto the field. It's something I haven't been a part of since sitting on the sidelines. I hate it. I hate not being able to be there for my team like I have been in the past.

I know it's not my fault, but I hate it, nonetheless. We haven't done well these last two weeks. Both losses. There's nothing like watching your team lose and not being able to do anything about it. I want to be out there on the field every Sunday. There's no feeling like it. And there's nothing worse than not being out there.

"Will you always be a kicker?" a soft voice in the back asks.

"Duh, Lily. You don't just change positions." The kid next to her has a lot of attitude.

"It's a valid question," I say, turning my gaze to Lily. "College players can change positions, but not so much in the NFL. I like kicking, so I won't change anytime soon."

She turns to the rowdy kid and sticks her tongue out at him. I hold back my laugh. It reminds me so much of Tenley and me that it puts a smile on my face.

Ever since we started this thing between us, every memory has taken on new meaning. How she was always there for me, high school and college, without question. How on some of my worst days, Tenley was the one I wanted by my side more than anyone else.

I answer questions as fast as the kids can shout them at me. They could rival any press we face after the game.

"Okay. I think that's all the time we have for today. Who wants to go with Miss Ashley to read?" Fifteen hands shoot into the air. "And what do we say to Mr. Jackson for coming in?"

"Thank you!" Tiny voices echo around the room before Tenley's teaching assistant takes them to another corner of the room.

"You're training new journalists here? These kids ask good questions."

Tenley gives me a proud smile. "I always tell them to be thoughtful before they ask questions. I don't want anyone's feelings getting hurt."

"Thanks for inviting me today, Tenley. Seeing you in your element is pretty badass."

"Shh! No curse words. I don't want tiny ears hearing them and repeating them." She slaps my chest.

"Sorry." I want to hug and kiss her before leaving but I can't. I settle for a wink instead. "See you at home?"

She backs away from me. "See you tonight."

And fuck if I can't wait for these next few hours to fly by.

Chapter Sixteen

TENLEY

"Why are we buying so many pumpkins?" Jackson asks, not for the first time today.

"Because every student needs to have one."

It's the perfect fall day. Wisps of white clouds stick to the bright blue sky. The snowcapped mountains loom large over us. With Jackson being more mobile now, I dragged him to the tiny farm outside the city.

"And what are you doing with said pumpkins?" Jackson heaves two onto his shoulders and puts them on the cart we have. It's hard to focus when his biceps flex like that.

"The students will paint them." I examine the two he put down and take one off. "Too many weird spots on this one."

"You're a perfectionist, you know that?" Jackson wipes a hand over his brow. The sun is beating down on us. The last of summer is holding on before we slide into October. Jackson is focusing more and more on getting back to football. I stole what might be one of his last free weekends to spend uninterrupted time with him.

I take his hand and pull him toward me. "You've met

my students. Do you think they'd settle for anything less than a perfect pumpkin?"

Jackson rests his hands on my waist. "Are we getting a pumpkin?"

We.

The word washes over me and settles in the vicinity of my heart. I don't think Jackson meant anything by it, but still. It makes me happy that he's connecting us in this way. Because I want to be connected to him in every way possible.

"Do you want to get one?" I lean back, staring into his squinty brown eyes.

"As long as we get to carve it. I don't want to paint it."

I laugh. "You do know we paint them because I can't give kindergartners knives, right?"

"I guess that makes sense."

I drop a quick peck on his lips and give him a gentle shove backward. "Now, go find good pumpkins, Mr. Fields, otherwise the consequences may be dire."

"Dire you say?" Jackson grabs my hand, pulling me back close to him. I get a whiff of his body wash. It sends tingles throughout my body.

"Dire." I give him a grim look.

"Well then." Jackson keeps his eyes on mine as he dips his head closer to my lips. "If the consequences are as you say, Miss Rhodes, then that kiss will not do."

In the middle of a pumpkin patch, Jackson lays one on me. It steals my breath as his tongue delves into my mouth. I don't care that it's the middle of the afternoon on a crowded Sunday. I can't get enough of Jackson. Of the way he takes command of this kiss. Like we'll both evaporate into thin air if we don't keep doing this.

Jackson pulls back first, the desire still swirling low in my belly.

"Right." He clears his throat, voice low with need. "I think that should keep any consequences at bay."

My brain is fuzzy as the world starts to come back into focus.

Jackson standing with his backward baseball hat.

The heated stare in his eyes.

His kiss-swollen lips.

What were we even talking about before?

"You need to stop looking at me like that, Tenley."

"Like what?" I nip at his lower lip.

His hands move lower, grasping my butt and pulling me into him. "Like you want to start something you can't finish here."

With a strength I didn't realize I had, I take two steps back. My head clears with a breath of fresh mountain air.

"Right. Pumpkins."

Jackson winks at me before pulling his sunglasses out of the V of his shirt and putting them on, effectively cutting off the haze of emotions around us.

"You best believe I'm finding the best pumpkin out here for us."

Turning on his heel, Jackson heads back into the patch, leaving me with only the thoughts of what a perfect day this is.

Jackson

"Are you sure you know what you're doing?" Tenley's tongue is peeking out between her pillow-soft lips.

"It's not the first time I've carved a pumpkin." She

doesn't look up at me as her knife gets stuck around the stem.

"Just because you've done it before doesn't mean you know what you're doing."

Tenley gives me an exasperated look, puffing out a breath of air as she pushes her hair out of her face. "Not all of us have biceps the size of tree trunks to help us."

"You mean these?" I flex my arms, giving her my cockiest smile.

"I'm surprised you're able to fit your head in the apartment." She rolls her eyes at me.

"It's why I keep you around. Always keeping me in check." I drop a handful of seeds and guts into the bowl. Tenley wanted each of us to carve our own. Something about a competition.

"You want some help?" I motion with the tiny carving knife in my hand.

She pierces me with her fiercest glare. "No. I don't want to win if you have to help me."

I laugh, shaking my head at her stubbornness. "Is this what you teach your students? If you can't do something, keep trying until eventually you give up?"

"Who says I'm giving up?" Tenley pops a hand on her hip, giving me what she thinks is her best attitude. If I measured up all of Tenley's attitude, it'd be the size of my pinky finger. She's quite possibly the kindest, sweetest person I know. As evidenced by the fact that she dropped everything to come and stay with me while I heal from my injury.

"Let me get you started." I reach for her knife, clasping her tiny hand in my much bigger one.

"Eww. Your hands are all gunky." She tries to pull back, but I don't let her. I squeeze even tighter.

"Let me help." I crowd her space, her ass hitting the

side of the table. Her pupils are dark, hiding the blue of her eyes.

"What exactly are you planning on helping with?" Her voice is husky now.

I spin her around, putting her hands where they need to be. "Just a little more muscle helping you carve." My lips ghost the shell of her ear.

Tenley relaxes into my hold. Her body is soft, compliant, against mine. I move my hand, the knife grating easily in and out of the pumpkin.

"Would you look at that?" Tenley turns her head a fraction of inch, her eyes meeting mine.

"That you're finally making some progress?"

The knife drops down as the circle on top of the pumpkin is complete. "Guess I needed you after all."

Tenley wiggles her hips against mine. It does nothing to help my hardening dick in my pants.

"You could've done this yourself the whole time, couldn't you?" I drop my lips to the exposed skin at her neck. My eyes watch as she pops the lid off, strands of seeds coming out.

"Jackson. I'm a grown woman. I can carve a pumpkin." She laughs.

Not paying attention to what she's doing, I take a step back right as a handful of guts is smashed into my face.

"What the fuck?" I wipe the goop off my face to see Tenley's bright smile right there. "Think you're funny, do ya?"

She shrugs a shoulder, sun-kissed from spending the day outside. "I mean, I guess so."

Scooping a handful off my nose, I shove it right back in her face.

"Eww! That went in my mouth!" She spits out the seeds as I reach for the pumpkin behind her.

"Serves you right."

I don't think Tenley has looked cuter than she does right now. But I don't let it distract me. Reaching into the pumpkin, I grab a fistful before smushing it in her hair.

"Oh, it is so on!" she shrieks. Tenley dives under the kitchen table, popping up on the other side. Grabbing the bowl of guts in her hand, she lobs a fistful at me. I try to duck out of the way with all the grace my knee will allow me, but she hits me square on the neck.

"Just so you know, you started this." The sticky goop creeps down the neck of my shirt. "Shit. This crap feels disgusting."

Tenley smiles back at me, so fucking proud of herself. Before she can move out of the way, I launch a handful at her.

Her laughter echoes around the small space as we try to dodge the other's attacks.

I can't remember a time when I laughed so much. Things with Rachel were always so fraught with tension. It was never easy with her.

But being with Tenley? We've slipped into these new roles together so easily. As if we were always meant to be together. Grabbing her around the waist, I pull her toward me, shoving some down her shirt.

"Okay, okay! I call a truce!"

Tenley tries to push off of me, but I hold tight.

"You giving up?"

"Jackson, I have pumpkin guts in parts of me no one should ever have. Yes, I'm giving up. You win."

"Damn. I didn't think I would."

I stare at the woman in front of me. Orange is smeared across her face, tiny fibers are stuck in her hair, and seeds cover her chest. I can only imagine how I look.

But the happy smile on Tenley's face hits me straight in

the gut. This woman is fucking gorgeous. She's wearing no makeup, and any other person would probably hide their face with how they look.

Not Tenley. She's plucking seeds off her as best she can, dropping them onto the table next to us.

"I guess I shouldn't have started something I couldn't win," she mumbles.

"If it helps,"—I grab a glob out of her hair—"you win the most beautiful award."

She laughs, shifting her gaze to look up at me. "Such a schmoozer."

Grabbing her chin, I force her eyes to stay on mine. "No. Just stating the truth."

Her eyes are alight with amusement as a blush creeps up her cheeks.

"You sure do have a way with words, Jackson Fields."

I shrug a shoulder. "What can I say? You just bring it out in me."

Tenley traces a finger down my jaw, eyes flitting over every part of my face. She looks like she wants to say something, opening and closing her mouth, but changes trajectory at the last minute. "Maybe we should get back to carving our pumpkins?"

I ignore the voice in my head, wondering what she wanted to say. Turning around, I scan the mess of the kitchen around us. One of the pumpkins fell to the ground, and our missed throws are splattered around every surface in the kitchen.

A deep belly laugh erupts out of me. "I think we're well past that point."

Tenley takes in the space, covering her mouth as she bends over in laughter. "I can't believe we did this."

"You started it." I point a finger in her direction.

She holds both hands up in defeat. "You didn't have to continue it. You athletes and your competitive nature."

"We don't like losing."

Tenley grabs one of the knives from the table. "Well then." She crosses the small, plastic knife over my shoulder. "I dub thee, Sir Jackson, knight of the pumpkin fight."

I love you. The words are on the tip of my tongue, but they get stuck, not wanting to get out. But this woman in front of me? I've never felt anything like this before. My heart is practically bursting in my chest thinking about this uninterrupted time we've had together.

As much as it sucks that it came at the cost of playing, I don't think I'd change it for anything in the world right now. Because getting to know all the different sides of Tenley has been the light at the end of the tunnel of this godforsaken road I've been on.

The tender side. The caring side. The sexy-as-fuck side. All of it rolled into my best friend in the world. One I can't imagine not ever having in my life.

Taking her hand, I drop the knife on the table and pull her toward me.

"I'll always be your knight in shining armor, Tenley. Always."

Chapter Seventeen

JACKSON

"You ready, Tenley?"

"Almost!" her sweet voice sings through the apartment.

My eyes sweep over the kitchen, her fingerprint on this place making it feel more like home than the past few years of living here.

A bright vase of flowers.

Books stacked on the coffee table.

Candles everywhere.

I never paid much attention to decorating. I don't spend much time here during the season. Even during the off-season, it's always workouts and team events, so the minimal décor never bothered me.

Not until Tenley moved in.

I know this is only temporary. That she's only here to help with my recovery. Hell, I'm getting around on my own now.

But I'm not ready to let her go yet.

"Sorry that took so long." Tenley comes to a stop in

front of me, adjusting the clasp on her bracelet. "Who knew coloring could get so out of hand today?"

I don't know if I could ever get sick of seeing her smile aimed at me. She's pure goodness. Too good for me some days.

She changed into a white short-sleeve dress, with a scoop neck that hints at what is below, with buttons down the front. It takes everything I have not to shove her back into the bedroom and unfasten every button and have my way with her.

"Stop looking at me like that." Her voice means business.

"Like what?" I feign innocence.

"Like you know what I look like naked."

I drop a kiss onto her cheek, getting a whiff of her sweet perfume. "I don't know what you mean." I kiss her other cheek. "You look beautiful."

Her cheeks flush as I pull back. Wrapping an arm around her shoulders, I guide her out of the apartment and to the elevator.

"Where are we going tonight?" Tenley walks into the waiting car, leans against the wall, and takes my hand in hers. Her fingers trace mine, putting me in a trance. The soft feel of her fingers against my rough hands sends a shudder across my body.

I pull her closer to me, her chest brushing mine. I don't miss her eyes widening in response.

I cup her cheek, my thumb skimming along her bottom lip.

"Larimer Square."

Tenley's fingers trace the collar of my T-shirt as a small smile plays on her lips. "Did you pick that for sentimental reasons?"

My brows pull together in confusion. "Sentimental reasons?"

A sigh escapes her lips. "I guess I shouldn't be surprised I remember more than you. It was the first time we hung out together without our parents after you moved in."

Dropping my forehead to hers, my lips find hers. The sweet taste that is Tenley lingers. I don't know how I ever could have confused her with Rachel.

"I like that you remember these things." My voice is soft as the elevator dings its arrival in the lobby.

Tenley shakes her head as we walk out of the building and make the short walk. "God, I was so gone for you back then."

"Only back then?"

Spinning in front of me, Tenley gives me another one of her smiles. The ones that are only for me.

"Eh. You're not so bad now."

"Not so bad?" I grab her, pulling her to a small alcove tucked away on the sidewalk. Pushing her back against the brick wall, her shocked eyes meet mine.

I don't wait. I don't ask for permission as I crush my lips to hers.

I swallow her whimper as she opens to me. Her hands cling to me. Steadying myself with a hand by her head, I wrap my hand in her hair to change the angle and deepen the kiss. Her tongue clashes with mine. Every ounce of need I feel for this woman is poured into this kiss.

Each kiss with Tenley is better than the last. Each kiss leaves me wanting more. More of her. More of her kisses.

Just…more.

I break the kiss, my lips hovering a breath from hers. "Not so bad?"

Her eyes are dazed. Her lips swollen from my kiss. It

has my dick thickening in my jeans at seeing her reaction to one hell of a kiss.

Tenley takes my hand and places it over her heart. The erratic beat is all over the place. "What does that tell you?"

Fuck. I am so screwed.

"DID you know this was going on?" Tenley's arm is linked through mine as we make our way through the crowds of people.

I shake my head as Tenley pulls me to a stop. The road is closed off for people drawing with sidewalk chalk. If I had known it would be this crowded tonight, I would've stayed home.

Sure, I get the usual people who recognize me, but being special teams, I'm mostly ignored.

But the thought of someone bumping into me the wrong way and hurting my knee more has my teeth on edge. Something like this never would have bothered me in the past.

For now, I'm plastering a fake smile on my face because I can't deny the joy it's bringing Tenley.

"This would be so fun to do with the kids." I love that Tenley is always thinking about her students. If there was anyone who was destined to be a teacher, it was her. She has the biggest heart of anyone I know.

Tenley is transfixed as she watches the artists in front of her. People are oohing and ahhing over their work. The Denver skyline highlights one drawing, while the quarterback for our team is in another.

"Think that looks like Young?" I nod to the drawing in question.

"It's a fairly good likeness." Tenley looks up to me, resting her chin on my bicep. "Think I could get them to draw you?"

I step back into the crowd, pulling her with me. "And on that note, let's get some dinner."

"Spoilsport." She sticks her tongue out at me as I open the door to the burger joint behind me.

"Trust me, no one wants to see me in chalk form."

Tenley tilts her head, taking me in. "I don't know. I'm sure they could do justice to all these muscles you have." She rests her hand on my stomach. "Besides, who would ever think to see you in sidewalk chalk?"

"Not me," I laugh.

"Did you ever think you'd be here?" Tenley asks as we settle into a booth.

"Hell no. I thought I'd be picked up by the last place team."

"Who would've thought…Jackson Fields, Denver's hometown kid, playing for the hometown team."

There's pride in her voice. Makes me feel ten feet tall.

"There's nowhere else I'd rather play."

A waitress comes by as Tenley and I talk about her day. About how close I am to getting to play again. It's then I notice two guys out of the corner of my eye.

"If our waitress comes by, will you get me another water? I need to go to the bathroom."

"Sure thing."

As soon as Tenley leaves, the two guys head my way.

"Jackson Fields, as we live and breathe." The taller one claps me on the shoulder like we're best friends.

"Hey man. Good to see you out and about. We need you," his friend chimes in.

"Thanks." I fight the grimace. This is one of the things I hate about playing. Everyone thinks they have access to you because you're a football player. A lot of people respect your time and space, but others waltz up to you without a care in the world.

"Ripley just isn't as good as you. He's not getting the job done." Plus they also say stupid shit like this.

"He's stepped up when we needed him." Do they really think I'm going to throw my teammate under the bus? "He's only a rookie and has been doing good."

This kid punches me in the shoulder. "You kicked twice as many field goals as him your rookie year. Dude needs to level up if he's going to be able to hang with the Mountain Lions. We need you back."

Who the hell does this kid think he is? It's not like I'm sitting at home twiddling my thumbs. "Can't rush this kind of injury."

"Pearson with Tennessee was back in under four weeks."

Before I can tell him where to shove it, Tenley appears behind them. "Sorry, where were we?" She doesn't sit, but stands next to the two idiots in front of me.

"Just talking about the game."

"Well, I'm ready to get back to our date. Do you mind?" Tenley gives them the sweetest, most fake smile that has them clapping me on the back and leaving.

"You okay?"

Whatever good feelings I had earlier about being out with Tenley tonight are gone.

"I'm fine. Let's just get the check and go home."

"We haven't eaten yet."

"Then let's get it to go," I snap.

Tenley crosses her arms, her eyes turning to steel. "They made you upset, not me. Don't take it out on me."

I go to counter her, but she flips a finger up at me. "I'd

think very hard about what you have to say before you say it."

My eyes drop to the placemat in front of me. With one single conversation, every thought I've had about my future with the team is questioned.

I'm not clueless as to how the new kicker has been performing. He's a rookie, thrust into the starting position much sooner than he ever planned on. It hasn't been a great start for the team, but it's not like we're 0-4. We're 2-2. Nothing to turn our noses up at. Yet it doesn't help the feeling like I'm letting my team down.

Everything I've been working toward my entire life has been football. Being sidelined these last few weeks has made me stir-crazy. I hate that I'm not contributing to the team. Putting doubt in the minds of our fans is the last thing I want to do.

"Let's go." Tenley doesn't wait for me as she makes her retreat from the restaurant. I follow her, the silence between us thick.

What was supposed to be a nice night out between the two of us turned sour. I hate how easily my mood changed, but it's been niggling at the back of my mind.

How easily I could be replaced and my football career gone with the single snap of a finger.

Chapter Eighteen

TENLEY

The apartment is dark as I shove the door open. All good feelings toward tonight, namely Jackson, disappeared in the blink of an eye. I could see the frustration on his face when those fans came up to him. I hate that people think they can come up and tell him things like that. It's not fair.

He deserves to be able to go out and do things without people telling him how much they need him back on the field. It's not like he chose not to play. It frustrates me to no end.

"Are you okay?" Jackson comes up behind me as I stare out the window.

"Fine." I cross my arms over my chest, not looking at him.

"I know you're not." His big hands land on my shoulders. "I'm sorry tonight didn't go as planned."

A sigh escapes my lips. "I just wish you wouldn't let them get to you."

"It's not that easy." Jackson wraps his arms around me, pulling me back into him. His hard body should overwhelm mine, like being wrapped in his protective cage, but not tonight. "It's even worse during losing seasons."

"It's a good thing you don't have a losing record then."

"Good thing." Warm kisses trail up my neck, setting my skin on fire. "But I really don't want to think about that when I have you in my arms."

I tilt my head to the side, giving him better access. "What would you rather be doing?"

A hand travels down my body, slipping between the buttons of my dress, fingers splaying across my stomach. The merest touch of his skin on mine has warmth gathering between my legs. A moan escapes me. Jackson's hard length is digging into my back.

"I want to lay you out on my bed. Undo each one of these buttons." His calloused fingers dig into my skin. "Taste your skin."

Damn Jackson. His words have me forgetting why I was mad at him. Mad at the situation we found ourselves in tonight.

"What are you waiting for?" My voice is breathless, filled with need for the only man I'd ever loved. Will ever love.

Breaking contact for the slightest moment, Jackson carries me to his room, laying me gently on his bed. He treats me like I'm a precious relic he doesn't want to break. Thank God his leg is strong enough to carry me.

"God. How did I ever get so lucky to be here with you?"

I feel Jackson's eyes everywhere on me. Shucking off his shirt and jeans, he crawls up the bed toward me. The faint lights of the city cast long shadows across his face. Brown eyes fill with desire as he takes my lips in a punishing kiss.

Wrapping my legs around his waist, I arch up to meet his touch. I ache to feel his body everywhere.

"Patience, Tenley. Patience." Jackson laughs against my lips. He pulls back, sitting on his heels. Those hands I love so much drift up the outside of my legs. Everywhere he touches sets my skin on fire, my soul on fire.

"You're exquisite." Jackson drops a kiss on the swell of my breast. "Stunning." Long, dexterous fingers find the first few buttons of my dress. Every pass of his fingers has me squirming beneath him. "The most beautiful creature I've ever laid eyes on."

His lips trail a path of heat down my chest and stomach as he undoes each button with care.

"I can't wait to taste you." Warm breath ghosts over the small swath of fabric covering my core. With my dress fully undone, Jackson pushes it to the side, kissing a trail back up the path he just traveled.

"Why are you teasing me? I need you," I whine. I shift, trying to find relief from the dangled pleasure before me.

I want Jackson in every way. I want his lips on my breasts, his dick inside me as he takes me to heights I've only ever experienced with him.

"I promise it will be good," he whispers at my ear. I whimper as he rocks against me.

"It's always good."

"Damn right it is." Jackson's voice isn't cocky, but confident as he strokes a finger down my covered core. "Every time is fucking phenomenal."

He slips a finger under the fabric of my underwear, the slightest touch nearly sending me over the edge. His knuckle hits my clit. "Jackson. Please."

"I like hearing you beg." Taking pity on me, Jackson sinks one digit inside me.

"I'll keep begging if it means more of this." I grab his wrist, holding him in place as he curls his finger inside me.

Jackson smirks as he pulls back, two fingers now moving inside me. I never thought it would be like this. Even the most casual of foreplay has me close to tipping over the edge.

It was never like this with anyone I'd been with before. Maybe it's because I never was fully invested in them. But with Jackson? Every time I'm around him, my body sizzles with electricity. The merest spark from his touch can light up my entire existence with a glow I've never felt.

I snake my hand up his chest, clasping the back of his neck and bringing his mouth toward mine. Our breath mingles as he picks up his pace.

"Jackson."

Tension coils tight within me as I try to hold on. But I can't. I clamp down on his fingers as my body lights up with an orgasm. Pleasure ripples through me, my body vibrating under Jackson's careful touch. Stars prickle the backs of my eyes.

"Fuck, baby. You look so good coming for me like that." My vision rights itself, Jackson coming back into focus. He's sucking my release off his fingers, his eyes heavy with lust.

I sit up, crashing my lips to Jackson's. The taste of my release on his mouth is heady. The feel of his velvet tongue against mine has me needing him again. I want another orgasm. I crave it.

When it comes to Jackson and orgasms, I'm greedy. I want everything he can give me. Tongue, fingers, everything. I want it all.

He pushes me back on the bed, his weight settling on top of me. My nipples are tight with anticipation. Wrapping my legs around his hips, I hold onto him, keeping him right where I want him.

The kiss slows, becomes less urgent, but no less intense. Each stroke of his tongue, each caress, is my undoing.

Running my hand down his chest, I rub it over the growing bulge in his boxers. Jackson rips his lips from mine, his forehead coming down against mine.

"If you keep doing that, I might come in my pants."

I can't stifle the giggle fast enough.

"You think that's funny?" His fingers find my side, tickling me. He rolls us over, me now on top of him, my dress fluttering against my sides. Laughter bursts out of me.

"I like that I turn you on that much." I rest my elbows on his chest, my fingers grazing through the scruff on his jaw.

Jackson stops tickling me, his hands grasping my butt under my dress, pulling me closer to him.

A softness washes over his face. "I hate that it took me so long to realize it was you. I feel like I'm playing catch-up."

My heart is close to bursting. I've never felt this way. After all those years of pining for Jackson, I never let my heart go. I kept it close, locked away for fear he would break it.

But now, it's out of its cage, feeling freely. It beats harder whenever Jackson is around. It swells more whenever he smiles at me. The softest caress has it ready to explode out of my chest.

I love that I finally get to experience these feelings with Jackson.

"Where'd you go?" His voice is a soft whisper as he tucks a stray strand of hair behind my ear.

"Thinking about you, that's all. How much you mean to me."

I drop a tender kiss over his heart, breathing him in. This man is part of me. As essential as breathing.

Jackson turns his lips up in a smile. "Let me show you how much you mean to me."

We move in silence, Jackson stripping off his boxers as I unfasten my bra and slip out of my underwear. Grabbing a condom from the nightstand, I roll it over his thick cock. I give it a few strokes, eager to feel him filling me, stretching me.

Jackson pulls me down to him, turning us so we're on our sides. Hitching my leg over his hip, he thrusts into me in one move. I cling to him, fingernails digging into his bicep as I adjust to his size.

A slight roll of my hips has his moving. Tiny shifts as he pulls out then slowly, inch by painstaking inch, sinks back inside me. His lips suck on the pulsing vein in my neck as heat rushes through me.

The care Jackson takes with me as he moves inside me has tears welling in my eyes. I find his lips, desperately trying to hold on to the last ounce of restraint with him. Jackson just got out of a relationship. I have no idea where this is going. My presence with him every day isn't necessary, but I'm not ready to leave him. Because only Jackson has the power to break me.

I'm too late.

And as he splits me wide open with another orgasm, I know I'm already lost to this man.

Jackson owns my entire heart, and I know I'll never get it back from him.

Chapter Nineteen

JACKSON

"Fiddlesticks," Tenley whispers under her breath.

"Everything okay?" Watching film has taken up most of my week. With the bye week upon us and an appointment with the team docs, I'm hoping I'll be cleared for the next game.

"Our field trip to the children's museum was canceled." Tenley plops down on the couch next to me. Strawberries and sunshine assault my senses. God, I can't get enough of the way she smells. It's permeated my entire apartment. Like it didn't know anything better before her.

"What happened?"

She rubs a frustrated hand through her hair. "Apparently a water pipe burst, and it's going to take them a while to clean up. So now I've got fifteen five-year-olds and nowhere to go."

I pause the game I'm watching. "Why don't you bring them by the team facilities?"

Tenley's eyes go wide. "Are you serious?"

"We've had kids there before. I don't see why it would be any different."

"I'm talking about this week, Jackson. There's no way they would let us come in only a few days."

Pulling out my phone, I shoot off a quick text to one of the team execs. "We can make it happen. Besides, if the parents sign off, we can post about it on social media. A little goodwill for the team. The press eats that shit up."

"I'd have to work with the school on that, but are you serious, Jackson?" A smile splits her face.

I pull her onto my lap. "Anything for you," I whisper against her lips.

I feel her smile as she wraps her arms around me. "You." Kiss. "Are." Kiss. "The best."

She leaps off me, grabbing her phone and starting to make calls. Her eyes don't stray far from me as starts talking logistics with someone.

That happiness on her face was from me. It makes my chest swell like a fucking caveman knowing I made her that happy.

My phone buzzes, letting me know the team will make it happen. I give Tenley a thumbs-up and she blows me a kiss in response.

Yup, fucking caveman.

"Okay, everyone. You all know Mr. Jackson."

Little faces stare up at me as Tenley talks to her students. I always thought kids would scare the ever-loving shit out of me, but I've had fun visiting Tenley's class the last few weeks.

"Is this where he lives?" someone shouts from the back.

Tenley gives them her best teacher smile. "This is where the Mountain Lions practice. And they're going to show us where they train and even let you run around on the field."

The parents chaperoning look more excited than the students. With what I have planned, I know they'll have fun.

"Is everyone ready?" I shout. A few shouts go up, but most of the kids just look confused. Looking behind the group, I see Alex, ready and waiting with the team mascot.

"That was pretty weak. Who's excited?" Alex yells and all the kids run to him.

"Wow. Am I chopped liver or what?" I ask Tenley as she sidles up beside me.

Her bottom lip sticks out and all I want to do is kiss her. "Poor baby. Don't like that Alex is getting all the attention?"

I cross my arms, giving her my best sad face. "What would you do to make it all better?"

We start walking onto the practice fields as Alex hands out footballs to all the kids. Lucky for me, all the captains live in Denver, so they weren't off to their beach houses for some sun on the bye week.

"I'd tell you that you are my favorite player." Her tone is dry.

"Way to be effusive with your praise." I roll my eyes as she laughs at me.

"Eh." Tenley shrugs her shoulders as she leans into me. "Quarterbacks don't do it for me. Kickers, though…perfection."

A smile tugs at the corner of my lips as she walks away from me. "Kind of how I feel about kindergarten teachers."

Knox and Colin are hanging back with some of the

other kids as Alex walks them through how to play the game. I've never seen so many sets of mesmerized eyes. I thought they'd all be bored playing, but I guess Alex can win over the toughest of crowds.

One of the girls in the class, Lily, is hanging toward the back of the group. "Everything okay?"

"I'm confused." She turns her big brown eyes on me.

"What's up, Lily?" I squat down to her level. For the first time in the last few months, it doesn't bring along agony. My knee feels good. And fuck, if that isn't the best feeling in the world.

"How come there are no girls on your team?"

"Uhh…" Oh shit. How do I answer her question without coming off like a huge dick?

"I mean, I like playing soccer because I'm a really good kicker. Do you think I could kick a football too?" She goes off on her own train of thought. "I kick the ball farther than my brothers, but they don't believe me."

"Lily!" A woman, I'm assuming her mother, hisses behind her. "He doesn't need to know all that."

I wave her off. "It's okay. Do you want to try kicking a football, Lily?"

Her eyes go wide. "Can I? I bet I could kick it really far!"

I stand and wave for her to toss me the ball she has in her hands. "Let's do it."

She chases after me as we walk over to the goalposts. Her mom has her phone out, clicking away at taking pictures. "Okay. Do you want me to show you how to do it, or are you ready to go?"

"I can do it!" She throws her tiny arms up in the air, as they peek out from beneath a sweater that's too big for her.

"I'll hold it for you and you kick."

I watch as she sets herself up. A few of the other kids

have started coming over to watch. She winds her tiny leg up and boots it about ten yards down the field.

"That was awesome, Lily! High five!" I hold my hand up for her, but she ignores it.

"But I didn't make it through."

"Do you think I made it the first time I tried kicking a field goal?"

"You didn't?"

I shake my head. "Nope. It took a lot of practice. Maybe if you keep practicing, you'll take my position one day."

"Okay! I'm going to practice really hard!" She chases down the ball as some of the other kids come over to try their hand at kicking.

I hold the ball as each one comes over before they go play with Alex. Soon, I'm all but forgotten as Tenley finds her way back to me.

"You know you're pretty cute with the kids, right?"

Her shoulder brushes mine. She mirrors my pose, arms crossed as we watch the guys try to corral the kids in a game. A few of them have taken to chasing our mascot around the practice field.

"They're good kids."

"You're not giving yourself enough credit. Not everyone can handle my kiddos."

Lily goes back to working on her kick. "It wouldn't surprise me if she makes it to the NFL someday." I nod in her direction.

Tenley turns to me, her eyes glassy. "Thank you, Jackson."

"It's no big deal."

"I'm serious." Her warm hand comes down on my forearm. "You really stepped up for me, and I know all of these kids are going to remember this day for a long time. This is special for them, and for me. So thank you."

Not many people can make me blush. One, in fact. I wish I could wrap her up in my arms and show her how much she means to me.

Instead, I step out of her bubble that always manages to suck me in. Football will clear my head, steer me back to safer territory.

"Anything for you, Tenley. Always."

Chapter Twenty

JACKSON

I'm so nervous I could puke. I'm more nervous than my very first game in the NFL.

Because today is the day. I'm hoping I finally get cleared to play this week. I've been working with Paige and our special teams coach to be sure I'm ready to go.

Every kick these last few days has felt good. Natural. Like I didn't miss a beat. And I'm hoping it pays off.

"You ready, Jackson?" The doctor comes in where I'm waiting on the table for my latest set of scans.

"Fuck, yes." I wince. "Sorry."

He waves me off. "Don't be. I'm used to it by now with a bunch of rowdy football players around all the time."

He sets the machine and I take a few deep breaths. The whirring of the machine is the only sound I hear.

I try telling myself that it'll be okay if I'm not back to full strength yet. Each injury is different and takes time to heal.

But fuck, it's hard. I want to be back out on the field. I want to hear the roar from the stands as we run out onto the field. When the fans cheer at a great play. And the thunderous applause when we win.

In other words, I want it all.

"Hang tight. I'll be back in a few minutes."

The doctor leaves the room and I'm shrouded in silence. I don't know if there's a worse feeling in the world than having to wait for news that could go either way.

I'm not left hanging long. Coach comes into the small room. A lead weight settles in my stomach.

"Fields. I hear you're waiting on some news."

"Oh God. They didn't send you to tell me the bad news, did they?"

He smiles at me. "Quite the opposite, actually. You ready to suit up Sunday?"

"You're serious?"

"I'm serious. Doc has given you the all clear."

"Oh thank fuck!" I sink back against the table, tears gathering in my eyes. I guess I didn't realize how much this was weighing on me.

"Let's get you back out with the team today. I know you'll want to go full-out today, but take it easy and listen to your coaches."

"Anything you say, Coach." My throat tightens with emotion. "I'm so happy to be back. It felt like this day would never come."

He claps me on the shoulder. "Everyone is happy to have our special teams captain back. Now let's go out there and show them how it's done."

I don't make it five feet into the apartment before Tenley is at my side.

"What did they say? Was it bad news? You didn't call me because it was bad? Oh God, I can't stand it." Her face is hidden behind her fingers.

"Nothing like that." I peel her fingers off her face. "It was all good."

"Really?" A slow smile spreads across her face. "You're playing next week?"

"I'm playing next week."

"Ahh!" Tenley leaps into my arms, peppering my face with kisses. "Jackson! I'm so proud of you."

Tears start leaking out of her eyes as she buries her face in my neck.

"There's no need to cry." Except my eyes are tearing up too. I squeeze her tighter.

"I know." Her voice is muffled. "I just can't believe that the day is here. You'll be playing next week. My stud of a boyfriend will be out on the field with the Mountain Lions."

"Boyfriend, huh?"

She pulls back, her eyes still glassy with unshed tears. "Is that not what we are?"

I set Tenley down on the back of the couch, towering over her. "Oh no, I like the sound of that. I just want to hear you say it again."

"My boyfriend is playing this weekend?"

"Fuck, do I like the sound of that from my girlfriend," I growl, burying my face into her neck.

Laughter, bright and happy, comes out of her. "Not as much as I like the sound of that."

"You better get used to hearing it often then, Tenley. Because as long as it makes you happy, I'm happy."

Chapter Twenty-One

JACKSON

"Are you ready for tomorrow?" Tenley crosses her legs under her as she watches me pack my bag.

I nod. "I am."

"And your leg feels good?"

I zip up my bag, getting ready to head out to the team hotel for the night. "Feels good. Feels strong." I can see her worrying her lip. "What's going on in that head of yours?"

Walking over to the bed, I cup her cheek, tilting her head up to me. Over the last few weeks, being with Tenley, I've started being able to read her emotions. They're written all over her face.

"I'm just worried. I know you'll be fine."

"I will be. They wouldn't let me play if I wasn't feeling good."

She gets up on her knees, wrapping her hands around my neck. "I feel like I have more skin in the game now if something happens to you."

"Oh yeah?" I quirk a brow, resting my hands on the curve of her ass.

Her hand drifts around, tracing my jaw. "I've never

been here for you like this after a game. I want you to go out there and win."

"Don't worry." I drop a soft kiss on her lips. "Whatever happens tomorrow, it'll be a win for me just being out there."

"I can't wait to see you play again. It's been too long."

I laugh, pulling her closer. "It's only been since last season."

Tenley smacks my chest. "And do you know how long the off-season is? Almost eight months!"

"Not for players."

"For fans it is. And I'm ready to see you play again."

I burrow my face into her neck, playfully nipping at her. "I'll make sure to make all of the field goals to impress you."

"You think that's what will impress me, Jackson Fields?" She laughs.

"I thought girls were into football players."

A soft look comes over her face. "Some girls, yes. But not me."

"Not you?"

"It's just what you do. There's a lot more I like about you."

"And what might that be?" I whisper against her lips. My fingers trail underneath the hem of her shirt. I need to get going if I'm going to get to the facility on time. But right now, I don't really care. Not when I have Tenley in my arms.

"I like how caring you are. How even though you act all tough, there's a softie underneath all of that."

"Only for you. Don't give away my secrets."

Her laugh is warm against my lips, and it has me seeking her mouth with mine. The soft whimper, the taste of her vanilla lip balm has me deepening the kiss. My tongue seeks her. Tenley's fingers tighten their hold on me as she pulls back.

"Shouldn't you be leaving now?"

"I wish I could stay here with you."

Tenley places a quick kiss on my lips. "I know. I also know how excited you are for tomorrow. So go. Go do your normal pregame rituals and kick some serious butt tomorrow."

I smirk—Tenley's lack of cursing always making me laugh. "See you tomorrow after the game?"

I pull back, feeling the loss of her heat immediately.

"I'll be the one sporting a number four jersey."

The thought of Tenley in my jersey has my dick hardening in my pants. Sure, she's worn it in the past, but that was before. Before we started this thing between us.

"You're killing me."

She blows me a kiss before I force myself to turn away from her. Like she said, as much as I want to stay with her, I'm ready to get out on the field tomorrow.

And kick some serious butt.

"FIELDS. HOW YOU FEELING?"

Our special teams coach comes up to me as I secure my pads before pulling my jersey on.

"Good. Ready. I can't fucking wait to run out there."

He smiles at me. "How sick of that question are you?"

"If it means I'm out there playing, you can ask me as much as you want." I laugh.

"Good."

"Alright, boys." The coach calls for our attention. "We ran through everything already. Washington is a strong team, so play your game and the rest will fall into place."

Shouts echo through the locker room as everyone files out, ready to run out onto the field. Everyone slaps the Mountain Lion on the wall before walking out.

Nerves tighten in my belly. It's been a long time since I've felt pregame nerves. I puked before my first college game. Before my first NFL game. Today feels different. I've never had to come back from an injury like this. Sure, I'll have the occasional aches and pains, but nothing that any player doesn't deal with.

Alex gathers everyone in the tunnel before we run out onto the field. "Okay, boys. Division game. Let's go out there and win this for our city, and for each other. And for Fields. Because who doesn't want a win their first game back?"

His words are drowned out by the sounds of the stadium before we all do our Mountain Lion chant.

Fuck, it feels good.

It feels even better when the team is announced.

Running onto the field, the grass hard beneath my feet, the fans chanting for us, those nerves are replaced with excitement.

There's nothing like game day. The energy that pulses through the stadium. The way the city all comes together on a Sunday to cheer for their team.

I stand on the sidelines as the American flag is unfurled to cover the field. Everything is moving by at light speed. Before I know it, we've won the coin toss and our defense is taking the field.

Washington is a good team.

We're better. And that's not me being cocky. Our defense is methodical in how they pick apart their offense. It's a thing of brilliance.

They get an easy three-and-out.

Adrenaline spikes. I always want touchdowns. Today though? Today I want to go out and put the first points on the board.

Our offense marches the ball down the field, but Washington stops us at their twenty-yard line.

Field goal time.

"Alright. Let's go!" Running out onto the field, I take a deep breath, centering myself. All my earlier nerves are gone. This is what I practice for. Kicking a football is second nature for me.

Our holder is in position to set the ball, looking at me for confirmation to snap it. Taking two steps back, I line myself up with the goalposts.

I'm ready.

Tapping my toe to the turf, I watch as the ball gets snapped and down in position. One step, two steps, and I'm swinging my leg and watching the ball sail straight through the uprights.

Fuck. That felt incredible. No pain in my leg. The familiarity of my leg connecting with the ball. Of seeing it sail through the air.

God, I live for this. There's nothing better.

I was worried I'd be rusty and that it'd be harder to shake off the cobwebs.

But it's like riding a bike.

Jogging off the field, I get slaps on the back as I find my seat on the bench.

"Looking good, Fields. Keep that up." I get a slap from the coach as I gulp down a Gatorade and resume my usual spot on the end of the bench.

Defense goes back to work. It shouldn't be so exhilarating watching our defense wreck their rookie quarterback, but I love it. I love seeing how each cog in the machine works.

Our defense stops them, sending our return team out onto the field. The stadium is electric. There's nothing stopping us today.

Young is tossing the ball on the field as my gaze shifts around the stadium. My eyes find the family suite.

My family has been to games before, but Rachel never came. Always had something better to do, she said. Having Tenley here today makes me want to play better.

I can feel her eyes on me from here. I smile into my cup as I think about seeing her after the game.

Our offense drives down the field with expert precision. An out route here, a twenty-yard run there. Offense is clicking today as they make the first touchdown drive look easy.

And it only continues from there after halftime.

I feed off our team's energy. Off the fans. Each kick gets better. Every time I get out there, my leg feels stronger.

And before I know it, the final whistle blows. Denver thirty-four, Washington ten.

The locker room is electric as we celebrate the win.

"Great win, boys, great win. Every aspect of the game was on point today. Offense, defense, special teams. And while we have a lot of great opponents ahead of us, let's celebrate today—but not forget what our ultimate goal is."

The assistant coach hands him a ball. "Today's game ball goes to our kicker. Fields, where are you?"

The guys crowd around me and shove me toward the center of the locker room. Any other day, I'd hate being the center of attention. But I'm feeding off everyone's energy today.

"You worked hard to come back, and you helped us

win today. So today's game ball is for you." He extends his hand, giving me the ball.

"Speech! Speech! Speech!" Everyone starts chanting around me.

"Alright, alright," I try to shush everyone, but they just get louder. "Thanks to everyone for your support. Today was a fucking awesome day, and I'm proud to be a Mountain Lion."

Whistles and cheers break out around me as everyone finally disperses. I answer questions for the waiting media before finally getting to hit the showers.

The adrenaline is pumping through my veins. And now that the game is over, there's only one person I want to share it with.

Changing back into my suit, I grab my bag and head to the family area. I zero in on Tenley immediately. I take her in, playing with some of the veterans' kids. My lips pull into a smile on their own. I don't go to her; instead I just watch her and the smile on her face as the kids chat her ear off.

When she finally spots me, her smile grows, if it's even possible.

"Jackson!" She launches herself into my arms. "You were amazing! Two for two on field goals, and all four extra points. Perfect."

The pride in her voice washes over me.

"It felt fucking good." I burrow my face into her neck, squeezing her tighter to me.

"And how's your knee feeling?" She pulls back, her face pink from the cold. A small Mountain Lion tattoo decorates one cheek.

"It's good. I iced it after the game, but it's good."

"You looked great. I'm so proud of you." Tenley takes my face in her hands and plants a loud smack on my lips.

"I couldn't have done it without you."

The pink in her cheeks deepens. "You would've been okay."

I shake my head. "I'm serious. Who knows where I would be if you weren't here helping me."

"There's nowhere else I would've been, Jackson." Tenley's fingers play with the buttons on my suit shirt as her blue eyes stare into mine.

Her pride, and something else, lingers there. It swirls deep in my belly. Right now, I'd rather be anywhere but here at the stadium.

"Are you ready to go?"

She nods, taking my hand and leading us out.

Because after a game like today, a perfect game, I want to spend the night with my favorite girl.

Chapter Twenty-Two

TENLEY

The door swings shut and Jackson is on me. His hand was on my leg the entire drive home. His long fingers kept drifting closer and closer to where I really wanted to feel them. The energy was alive and buzzing in the car.

It exploded the second we made it into Jackson's apartment.

"Fuck. You look so good in my jersey." Jackson lifts me against the wall, his hands moving under the jersey sporting his number. "So fucking sexy."

Warm kisses move down my jaw, sucking and nibbling. His hard length pulses between my legs as I cling to him.

"You were incredible today." Finding the silky locks of his hair, I hold on to him. "You were a man possessed."

Jackson pulls back, lust and desire clouding his eyes. "I liked knowing you were there watching me."

"Did that make you want to play better?"

A cocky smirk paints his face. "Would you judge me if I said yes?"

I shake my head. "No. I like that you want to impress me. Not that you have to."

I lean down, sipping on his lips. Nibbling on his bottom lip. Heat pools between my legs as Jackson takes control of the kiss. Despite the cold afternoon, my skin is on fire, alive with need as Jackson walks us into his bedroom.

Dropping me on his bed, Jackson's eyes rove over me. I feel them everywhere. Goose bumps break out on my skin. Everywhere they look, they brand me like a hot iron.

"I've been dying to have you under me." Jackson nudges my knees apart as he settles over me. A hand runs up the outside of my leg, but his eyes don't leave mine. He is a man with one focus. Strong fingers undo the button on my jeans and pull the zipper down. But Jackson doesn't do anything else. He hovers over me.

His pupils are dark with lust. My tongue slips out, wetting my lips. The bulge behind his pants is obvious.

Jackson settles his weight between my legs, and I let out a moan, feeling him against my own aching core. The scent of his body wash lingers as his lips find my neck.

"God, you taste amazing." I shift under him, wanting to feel more of his skin on mine. "Why is it so intoxicating to see you like this?" He pulls back, running a hand down my side and fisting my jersey.

The possessive look in his eyes stills me. I've never seen him like this. The Jackson I've always known and loved has never been good at showing his emotions.

But this one is showing me everything. And the growl that rumbles from his chest as he takes me in another life-altering kiss?

It's possessing. Claiming.

And in this moment, I want to give myself over to him. To let him own me. Worship me. Dominate me in every way.

Jackson pushes the thick jersey and the T-shirt under it up and over my head. My nipples pebble under his heated stare. Lifting me into the center of the bed, Jackson's lips close over the thin material of my bra.

A moan breaks free. "Oh Jackson."

Big hands skirt down my stomach, and wetness gathers between my legs. When his hand finally pushes under the material, and his fingers find my clit, I have to bite down on my lip to keep from coming.

"Feel good?" Jackson asks, kissing the swell of my breast.

"You know it does." My voice is breathless as he peels the cup of my bra down and takes my other nipple in his mouth. Between his lips on me and his fingers sliding through the wetness of my core, I'm close to exploding.

"So good. So, so good." Arching off the bed, I lean into his touch as his mouth moves back up my chest. Hot kisses sear into my skin, burning into my soul. Each one marking me as Jackson's.

Because as Jackson sinks a digit deep inside me, it hits me with a clarity that I haven't felt in a long time.

I'm Jackson's.

Completely and wholly.

I've always wanted to be his, but never was.

And now that I am, I know that I never want to lose this man.

My orgasm hits me with a quiet force. I cling to Jackson, riding it out as his forehead dips to meet mine. The power of it has tears welling in my eyes.

"Tenley." It's a prayer coming from his lips.

I wrap an arm around his shoulders, anchoring myself to him as waves of pleasure roll through me.

"God, you're fucking sexy when you come."

He pulls back, dark eyes roaming over my body. It

draws out my orgasm that much longer. Jackson stands, shrugging out of his clothes, his hard length protruding straight out. I lick my lips in anticipation.

I watch as Jackson rolls a condom on. His weight on top of me is the most delicious feeling in the world. The way his chest brushes my nipples. The way his hands drift along my stomach makes it dip in anticipation.

"Please, Jackson. I need you."

His kiss-swollen lips crash to mine as he enters me in one slow thrust.

I'll never get used to the feeling of Jackson being inside me. Every time he fills me feels better than the last. Our bodies come together in the perfect rhythm. I meet every thrust before he drags his hard length out, waiting before pushing back in.

Sweat gathers on his brow as he hikes my leg up higher on his waist. "Fuck. This feels amazing."

Jackson's words are mumbled against my neck. My fingers find purchase in his back as he continues his thrusts. They're no longer slow and controlled, but hard and fast.

Each roll of his hips is hitting a spot deeper and deeper inside me. The heat coiling in my center is ready to explode.

"I'm so close."

"I'm there, Tenley. I can't hold on any longer."

His release fills the condom, triggering my own. His thrusts slow as he holds me through our release. I feel every bit of this orgasm in every part of my body. It rearranges my very essence and imprints itself into me.

Jackson has stamped himself on every part of me as he collapses on top of me. Our breaths mingle as our bodies come down from the earth-shattering experience we just shared.

"Holy fuck, Tenley. I think I blacked out for a minute there."

I drag my fingers through his hair, his words causing a flutter in my belly. "Mmm, I know what you mean. That was…"

There are no words to describe how powerful that orgasm was.

"I know." Jackson presses a kiss to the swell of my breast, over my heart. The very place where the man has taken up residence.

Never in my wildest dreams did I think things could be like this with Jackson. He's everything and more.

I only hope we can continue like this, because with him playing again, football will take center stage again.

I hope it's a limelight that we can share.

A
B
C

Chapter Twenty-Three

TENLEY

"So who are we cheering for in this game?" I take a bite of the pizza as the late game drags on. It's 0-0 in the second quarter, neither team looking great.

"As much as I hate to say it, Vegas. We need them to win so we're one game closer to Kansas City in the playoff run."

I shake my head, water droplets from my earlier shower landing on the T-shirt I'm wearing. "I will never understand playoff seeding."

Jackson turns toward me. "Tenley, I don't even think most players understand who has to lose what game by how many points to make it when it's close."

His playful smile tells me all I need to know. Jackson's fingers trace circles back and forth on my exposed leg. The adrenaline was flowing when he got back after the game. Not that I was complaining. I relish any chance I get to be with Jackson.

We're well into the season and the Mountain Lions have a fighting chance at the playoffs.

"Still. It doesn't make me like having to cheer for them."

Jackson turns toward me, a lazy smile on his face. "It's for the good of Denver."

I squeeze his bicep. "Well then, I will be annoyed on your behalf. I hate the guy who did this to you." My eyes find the now-melted bag of ice on the bed. Taking my last bite, I throw the crust into the empty box and wipe my hands.

"I like this side of you."

"Oh yeah? And what side is that?" I trace a finger up and down the prominent vein in his arm.

"The protective side of you." He squeezes my thigh, and a bolt of lust swims through me.

I situate myself over him, his eyes darkening. "It doesn't mean I have to like you getting injured and then having to cheer for that team."

Jackson squeezes my butt, pulling me closer to him. My hands land on his hard pecs as I breathe him in. The scent of his soap is all consuming.

"I like having you on my side." His hand drifts up my side, coming to rest on the beating pulse in my neck.

"You've always had me on your side." I drop my forehead to his.

Jackson's thumb brushes my lower lip, eliciting a small moan. "But I like getting to see this side of you."

"Do you think we would have made it?"

"If we started dating in high school?" Jackson finishes my thought.

I nod.

He pulls back as the sounds of the game quiet around us. "Honestly? I don't know. What if we ended up like Rachel and me?"

"I don't know if we would have ended up like that. But I don't know if I would have been ready for you."

A small smile plays on Jackson's mouth. "Fuck, I know I wasn't. I think part of the reason it was so easy to be with Rachel was because we weren't actually in love."

"Really?" My brows tighten in confusion.

Jackson leans back against the headboard, his hands trailing down my thighs.

"By the time I realized in high school I could be good enough to get a scholarship for football, I was nothing more than a means to an end for Rachel. I think it's why I focused so hard on football and being good enough to get to the NFL."

"So why didn't you end things with her when you were drafted?"

"Jersey chasers." Jackson laughs.

"Oh yes. The sexy Jackson Fields. Women would've been throwing themselves at you."

"You laugh, but it's true." Jackson points a finger at me.

Grabbing it, I link our hands together. "So you stayed with Rachel out of convenience?"

"I'm not proud of it, but we both used each other in a way. Her to get ahead, and me to not have to deal with the lifestyle that comes with being an NFL player."

I want to ask what this means for us. But this is still so new. The change from friends to more than friends was seamless. Almost too seamless. Am I just something to occupy Jackson's time?

"Thinking some pretty heavy thoughts there, Tenley." Jackson smooths a finger between my eyes.

"And what makes you think that?"

"Because I know you."

"You do." I take in the face that I've been in love with

for what seems like as long as I can remember. I barely remember a time when I didn't love Jackson.

"So what's on your mind then?"

"Everything happened so fast between us."

"And you're worried about that?"

I nod. "I'm just worried about what might happen next."

In a flash, Jackson has me on my back, his weight settling on top of me. "That's not something you have to worry about."

His nose drifts along mine, his breath warm against my face. Whenever we're together like this, desire throbs in my veins. I should be used to it by now.

"No matter what, Tenley, it'll always be you and me."

My heart threatens to burst out of my chest at Jackson's words. I thought I loved this man before. But it's nothing compared to now.

I capture his lips with mine in a slow, sensual kiss. The slide of his tongue against mine sets my entire body on edge. I want more with each pass of his tongue against mine.

I've never ached for someone like this before. Every cell is vibrating with need for this man. To feel every part of him against every part of me.

"I love the way you taste." Jackson pulls back, taking my face in one hand. "I love the way you look at me. The way you smell. God, I love it all."

"Mmm, Jackson."

It's not the words I want to hear from him, but he yearns for me just the same. Wrapping my legs around him, it feels like I might incinerate if I don't feel him inside me.

Jackson pushes my shirt up and over my head, exposing my naked body to him. He growls in response.

"Fuck." Jackson sucks on my neck, wetness gathering between my legs. My nails scrape down his back, skirting with the waistband of his sweats.

"I need you, Jackson."

A trail of wet kisses burns hot down my neck. My chest. "In time, Tenley."

He takes a nipple in his mouth. "I love your mouth on me."

"Mmm, I love how responsive your body is to me." Every inch of skin breaks out in goose bumps. Tension swirls in the air around us.

Jackson kisses his way to my other breast, tugging at the diamond-hard nipple. I roll my hips under him, seeking more. His own desire is hard against me.

His lips move down my body, a whisper against my skin before he pushes my legs apart. His eyes find mine, a playful look there as his tongue darts out between my folds.

"Gah!" It's too much. It's not enough. He devours me with his fingers and tongue, ratcheting up my pleasure. I'm a writhing mess beneath him as my orgasm nearly splits me in two.

Stars appear behind my eyes as lightning heat takes over my body. It burns bright as Jackson works me through one of the most intense orgasms I've ever experienced. I never knew sex could be like this. Maybe it's because I'm with someone I love and who cares for me that it's this good.

My breath comes in gasps as my body comes back down to earth.

"You are the most beautiful woman when you come undone like that," Jackson whispers into my mouth. "It will be burned into my brain forever."

I open my eyes, taking in the heavy lust in Jackson's. I

pull him up my body as his naked skin meets mine. Not a whisper of air could get through.

"I want you inside of me."

Jackson goes to reach for a condom, but I stop him. Telling him without words that I want nothing between us.

"Are you sure, Tenley?"

I nod. "Yes. Please."

Jackson crushes his lips to mine, my own release lingering there. I wrap my arms around him, wanting him closer, but with nowhere to go, Jackson pushes inside me in one quick thrust.

He swallows my gasp, stilling inside me.

"I don't think I'm going to last." His words are hot against my neck. "You feel too good."

I pulse around him, still reeling from my first orgasm. "Then start moving."

Jackson's thrusts are long and hard, hitting a spot inside me that steals my breath. Sweat gathers on my brow as I try to stave off my second release of the night. I want to savor the feel of Jackson bare inside me.

Nothing has ever felt so good. So right.

Jackson pushes up on his elbows, his eyes raking over me in a way that makes me feel cherished. I link my hands behind his neck and pull him down.

"I need you to come. Fuck, I need to come."

Every move of Jackson's hips is getting harder, faster. His fingers skate down my stomach, finding my clit. One, two strokes and I'm coming undone.

I feel like a woman possessed at how easily I come apart for Jackson. I've never felt so much, like my body might explode because it has nowhere to go.

Love. Pleasure. Ecstasy.

"Tenley." My name is a growl on his lips as I feel him come inside me. It drags my own pleasure out. Electricity moves around us as Jackson takes me in his arms and flips over to his back.

"How are you feeling?" Jackson huffs out after who knows how long. Our bodies cool as we stay together, neither making any move to leave.

"Happy. Sated."

"That all?" Jackson drags a finger down my arm.

"Something else I should be feeling?" I burrow myself into his arms, kissing the hard muscle under me.

Jackson slips out of me, moving down the bed so we're eye to eye. The look in his eyes steals my breath from me.

"Love?"

The colors of the TV play across his handsome face in the dark room.

"I know it might seem fast, but I love you, Tenley."

"Yeah?"

Jackson tucks a lock of unruly hair behind my ear. Every time he touches me feels like the first time. It's like he's permanently electrified my body whenever he is near. I don't want to lose this feeling.

"It took me a little longer to realize that it should have, but I do." Jackson takes a nervous breath. "I didn't recognize what I was even feeling because I've never felt like this."

"I know what you mean. I've only ever felt like this for one man."

Jackson growls. The predatory look in his eyes tells me he has no idea who I'm talking about. "I don't want to know about him."

"You don't?" I push Jackson onto his back, hovering over him.

"No." Another growl.

"That's a shame." I drag a finger down his nose. Over

the Cupid's bow in his lips. Across his jaw. "Because I love talking about him."

Understanding dawns in his eyes. "Tell me about him."

Settling his arms behind his head, his eyes focus on me. "He can be kind of grumpy sometimes."

"I'm not grumpy."

I press a finger to his lips to quiet him. "He doesn't take criticism very well either, apparently. I'm learning some new things."

His jaw tics as he sucks the tip of my finger in his mouth.

"He supports me, even though he was fighting to make it back onto the field."

Jackson runs a hand up my leg, pulling me down to him. "Tell me more."

"He's a pretty good kisser. And an okay kicker."

"I take back everything I said."

Laughter bursts out of me as Jackson tickles my side, moving over top of me. "Have you always been this feisty?"

"I guess you bring it out in me." I try to push him away, but he holds on tighter. I'm fighting for breath as he rocks back on his heels.

"Take it back."

"Which part?" I sit up, not backing down from him. "I don't think I said anything that wasn't truthful."

"You're lucky I love you, Tenley."

"Yes, I imagine it must be so hard to put up with someone like me."

Jackson rolls off the bed walking toward the bathroom, the low lights of the TV highlighting the fine physical specimen in front of me.

"Hey." I get on my knees, crawling over to him. Wrapping my arms around him from behind, I whisper the words I haven't yet said to him. "I love you, Jackson. I have for a long time and will continue for a long time going forward."

Jackson's warm hands land on my arms. "I don't think I'll get tired of hearing you say those words to me."

I press a warm kiss to his neck. "Then I'll tell you every day. I love you. I love you. I love you."

Happiness and warmth spread through me as Jackson turns in my arms. "I love you. Now I'm pretty sure we both need some sleep because we've got long days ahead of us."

Wrapping me in his arms, Jackson moves us both back on the bed, pulling the sheets up around us. His quiet strength seeps into me as he turns the TV off and we settle into each other's arms.

I could get used to this, hearing those words I've longed for from him since ninth grade. Sleep takes over, a smile on my face, as I think about how perfect life is in this moment.

Chapter Twenty-Four

JACKSON

"Jackson. Can I see you in my office?" Coach's voice echoes around the weight room. I drop the bar I'm working with and follow him out of the room to stares from the guys. It's like being called to the principal's office.

"What's up, Coach?"

Sweat drips from every pore as I stand in his office, waiting for the bad news that is written all over his face.

"Have you seen the news?" He throws a magazine down on his desk. A picture of Rachel and me glares up at me under the headline *Fields's Ex Tells All—is he really a selfish lover?*

"Oh for fuck's sake. Are you serious with this shit?" I toss the magazine in the trash can next to his desk. I drop into the seat, frustrated at the turn my day has now taken.

"As much as you don't want to deal with it, you have to." Coach has always been one of the more patient people I've worked with. He never raises his voice and is the calm and steady influence in the locker room.

"Even if all of it is crap?" I don't have to read it to

know that it's all lies. Rachel was one to bend the truth to her liking to get what she wanted.

Coach's lips pull into a thin line. "It usually makes the person they talk about look bad. Even if it's all lies, we'll have the team issue a statement."

I roll my eyes. I should've known Rachel wouldn't go quietly. As much as she's gained her own popularity as an influencer, I was an easy meal ticket for her.

"And what if that doesn't work?"

Coach shrugs his shoulders. "Then we'll cross that bridge when we get to it. For now, I want you to focus on your game. Buffalo is coming up this weekend, and they're on a hot streak."

I nod, trying to push the article out my head. "You got it."

Standing, I head back to the weight room to finish my reps. Except my focus is shot. I don't give two shits about what Rachel said about me. It's all lies. My biggest concern is Tenley and what she'll think of it.

Because the last thing I want is her being affected by this.

Tenley

"ARE YOU OKAY?" Jackson's deep voice stirs me out of my angry cutting.

She looks up, her worried blue eyes meeting mine.

"Why wouldn't I be okay? I only had to read about your sex life with Rachel—in detail, mind you—only a few hours before my family comes over for dinner." I plaster on a fake smile. "Totally okay."

"Fuck," Jackson whispers. "You know none of that is true, right?"

I drop the knife, ignoring the dinner I should be finishing. "Does it matter if it's not? It's still out there."

Jackson comes around the island, approaching with caution. "The team put out a statement."

"Oh good. Because then everyone will ignore the fact at how you take and take in bed and give nothing back."

Jackson steps back like I slapped him. "Well that's not fucking true and you know it."

Rubbing the heels of my hands into my eyes, I try to quell my rising emotions. Anger. Jealousy. Worry. More anger. "I know. But why would she do something like this?"

"I love how you see the good in everyone." Jackson wraps his arms around me. For the first time today, the anger dissipates.

"Is it always going to be like this?"

"Going to be like what?" Resting his chin on my shoulder, I sink into Jackson's hold.

"Worrying about someone dragging you through the mud. Some scandal I don't know about waiting to rear its ugly head. Fans yelling at you when we're in public."

"It's an up and down season. It comes with the territory."

"A territory that I have no idea how to navigate."

"What's really going on, Tenley?"

Before I can answer, the door buzzes. Jackson releases me but doesn't take his eyes off me. "We're not done talking about this."

I follow him, a fake smile adorning my face for the second time today.

"Hi, sweetheart." My mom's chipper voice greets me.

"Hi, Mom." I wrap her in an extra-long hug, needing all the strength I can muster to get through tonight.

"Something smells good."

Jackson stands with my dad, making easy conversation as my mom and sisters follow me into the kitchen. Sadly, my nieces and nephews had soccer practice with their dad tonight, so there's no one to divert attention away from me.

"How are you doing?" Penny asks, going to pour the bottle of wine I have set out.

"Fine. Why?" I shrug a casual shoulder, not wanting to show just how flustered I am today.

"You know why." Nora pins me with a glare over her glass.

"Can we please not talk about this?" It doesn't surprise me my sisters found out. But I have zero desire to discuss this with them or anyone else right now.

"Talk about what?" My mom glances between the three of us in the kitchen.

"Rachel released a tell-all about her and Jackson's sex life," Nora says without pause.

"Seriously?" I gulp down half the wine in my glass. "You had to tell Mom?"

"It's not like I wouldn't have found out." She pins me with a stare only a mom can use.

Glancing around her, my dad and Jackson are occupied in the living room. Thank God. The last thing I want is my dad to be here for this conversation.

"It's not like Mom is great at technology. She might've missed it entirely," Penny states, so matter-of-factly.

"I'll have you know I learned how to set up my own gram account the other day." She gets a hoity look about it.

"You mean Instagram, Mom?" Nora quirks a brow at her.

She points back at her. "Yes. That. I did it all on my own without having to call you for help. Now, what's this article all about?"

Nora dives right in, telling her, in excruciating detail, about what Rachel said about their sex life.

"Well, it can't all be true." Mom shrugs her shoulders and makes herself at home, starting to plate dinner for everyone.

"And why is that?" Nora asks.

"Tenley wouldn't be with anyone who is selfish and doesn't think of others. She has too good a heart."

My insides settle at my mom's words. "Thanks, Mom."

I help her set the table as my dad and Jackson come into the room.

"How's school been, Ten?" Dad's voice booms throughout the small space. He's loud. He needed to be to be heard with four women in the house growing up.

"I've got a great group of kids this year." I wrap an arm around Jackson's waist as he sidles up to my side. "They love this guy."

"I was telling your dad that I had been to visit your class before I started back with the team." Jackson wears a proud smile. "I like getting to see you teach."

"Tenley's the best there is," Dad says, as we all sit down around the table.

"I happen to agree." Jackson sits down next to me, his smile still plastered on his face.

"Ugh, gross." Penny rolls her eyes from across the table.

"Penny." Dad's voice is firm. "You can still be happy for your sister."

"I am happy for her. Doesn't mean I need her new relationship thrown in my face."

The annoyance in her voice is plain as day. Only sisters can get away with that.

"Don't pay any attention to them." My dad waves us off, turning his attention to Jackson. "How are things going with the team? Denver's looking good."

"We've got a hard stretch in front of us. Hopefully we'll be able to keep the momentum going."

"Denver needs a Super Bowl. It's been too long," Dad states matter-of-factly, shaking his head.

Jackson's lips tighten. "That's what we're hoping for too."

Conversation is light after that. Jackson has been around my family since they moved in next door. I'd spend days at his house, and he'd come over to mine. It's the balm to an afternoon of frayed nerves.

All too soon, everyone starts making their way to the door. My mom stops me before I can follow.

"Are you going to be okay?" Mom cups my cheek.

I bite my lip to keep from crying. The emotions of the day have taken their toll. "I'll be fine."

"It's okay to slow things down, Tenley."

"Why would we need to slow things down?"

Her lips draw into a tight line. "You've only just started this new relationship with him. It's okay to get to know one another. Guard your heart."

I step out of her hold, my defenses going up. "Why would I need to guard my heart?"

"Sweetheart, I don't mean it in a bad way. You're the kindest, most loving and caring person I know. I don't want to see you get taken advantage of."

"Jackson won't take advantage of me." Crossing my arms, I try to keep my anger from boiling over.

"He might not, but he's in the spotlight whether you

want him to be or not. And most people won't think twice before stepping over you to get to him."

Her words pull at the string that I've been trying to ignore all afternoon. This is a side of Jackson that I've never experienced. The side that comes with football fame. Today it's Rachel, tomorrow it could be anything.

Jackson has always been my best friend. It's a role I've been comfortable with. I was never in the spotlight like him and Rachel. But now, any future with Jackson means I'm there too. It's a place I've never been, and a place where I don't want to spend my time.

But if it means being with Jackson, can I handle it?

It's a question that I don't want to look at too closely, because the answers might not be what I want them to be.

Chapter Twenty-Five

JACKSON

"You ready for the game tomorrow?" Tenley tucks her hands under her head as she faces the camera on her phone. Even though she doesn't have to be staying at my place with me gone, she is.

It's been a long week for the two of us. The article Rachel released hasn't died down, and I hate seeing the toll it's taken on Tenley.

"I am."

"And your knee feels good?"

I smile at the care in her voice. "Always worrying about me."

"Someone has to make sure you're taking care of yourself."

"Oh yeah?" I give her a sly smile. "And who's taking care of you?"

"No one that's here right now." She quirks a brow at me.

"Just because we're apart doesn't mean I can't take care of you."

I don't miss the flare in her eyes. "And how do you plan to do that?"

Wetting my lips, I focus my gaze on the tiny camera that holds the woman I love. "Take off your shirt."

A blush pinks up her cheeks. "Are you serious? We can't…do that."

"Why not?" It's one perk of being a captain. We get our own room when we travel. I move closer to her, as if it will make her magically appear in my bed.

Tenley bites her lip, giving me a shy smile. I know what lies beneath that good-girl facade. "Because I've never done it before."

Her confession has a smile slipping across my face. "Would it make you feel better if I told you I'd never done it before?"

"Really?" Tenley's voice kicks up a notch as I nod at her.

"So don't make me ask again."

This time, Tenley hesitates only a moment before taking off her shirt. Dusty-rose nipples are already diamond hard. My dick is ready to burst through my sweats at how turned on she is.

"What do you want me to do next?"

The desire in her voice drives my hand beneath the waistband of my sweats, taking my cock in hand. Precum drips from the tip.

"Play with your nipples."

Tenley adjusts the camera, setting it up next to her. Slender fingers tweak at her nipples, and it pulls a groan from deep inside me.

"I wish you were here doing this," Tenley whispers.

"What do you like about it?" My hand is rough as I jerk myself off.

"I love how strong your hands are." She plucks a nipple between her fingers, back arching off the bed.

"Does it make you wet?" I growl.

"Mmhmm."

"Show me," I demand.

Tenley doesn't waste a second. Her hand disappears below her underwear.

"Fuck. I wish I were there." My focus is singular, not taking my eyes off the phone as Tenley's fingers disappear.

"Gah!"

The sounds coming from Tenley push me that much closer to the edge. Setting the phone down, I push my sweats down, my balls drawing up tight, ready to explode.

"Let me see you," Tenley asks, voice breathy.

Flipping the camera, I give her an up-close-and-personal view of my leaking dick. The head is an angry purple. "I wish it were your hands on me."

My hips jackknife off the bed. Tenley's quiet moans and gasps are the only sound echoing around the quiet room. We move together, both of us quiet, as we get closer and closer to release.

"I'm close, Jackson." Tenley shoves her underwear down, angling her hips so I can see that beautiful pussy of hers.

It's like I'm a man possessed. Seeing the evidence of how turned on Tenley is has my hand moving faster. "I'm right there with you."

"Jackson!" Tenley's yell through the phone is staticky as the phone falls. Her panting breaths push me over the edge, spilling into my hand and all over my stomach.

"Fuck, yes!" I work myself over as sticky ropes of cum land on me. "Fuck, that's so good."

Tenley's face appears in the tiny box, sated and happy. "Jackson?"

"Mmm, yeah?" It's late now, with me traveling this afternoon and then sitting through back-to-back team meetings once we landed.

"I liked that."

Wiping the mess off my stomach, I turn and set the phone on the bed, mirroring her position. "I did too."

"Kind of makes the away games worth it."

"I miss you," I confess. It's never felt like this before when I traveled. Before, I reveled in the peace of being on my own. But now, my attention is split. I want to be with Tenley but know where I need to focus. Football and the big AFC matchup tomorrow.

"Luckily you'll be home soon. And I know you're going to kick butt tomorrow."

I smile at her confidence in us. "Buffalo is a good team. It'll be a hard game."

Pulling a sheet over her naked body, Tenley settles back against the headboard. "I know, I know. You don't want to jinx yourself. But me saying how well you'll play tomorrow isn't going to affect your performance."

"Athletes are a superstitious bunch."

"I know. Now, you need to go get some sleep."

I sigh, looking at the time on the alarm clock. "I love you." The words come so easily to me now. I want to tell her every chance I get because Tenley deserves to hear them as often as possible.

"I love you. Good luck tomorrow."

Tenley blows me a kiss and ends the call. Blowing out a breath, I think about the woman on the other end of the line.

We slipped so easily into this new thing between us that it almost seems too good to be true. But each day with Tenley is better than the last. And for the first time in my life, my sole focus isn't football. I should be more worried about how easily she pulled my attention away from football, even with all the noise in the background.

Spending time with Tenley is only adding more balance to my life. I keep that front and center as sleep finally pulls me under.

"THAT WAS A TOUGH LOSS TODAY, boys. It's no one's fault."

That's the understatement of the century. The howling winds and rain in Buffalo today were no match for us. We're used to playing outdoors, but this weather was shit.

Two missed field goals and an extra point. And that wasn't even the worst of it. Buffalo's D had two pick-sixes. We looked like a joke out there, like a peewee team that had never played a down of football before.

"Decompress tomorrow, and then we'll take a look at the film on Tuesday."

A few mumbles are heard before he heads back to the office. There's nothing worse than a tough loss. Especially on the road. It'll be a long flight back to Denver tonight.

The locker room is quiet as guys go through their postgame routine. Dropping my pads into my locker, I head back to the therapy area, needing an ice bath for my knee.

"Feeling okay?" Alex is getting his shoulder looked at after a hard hit in the fourth quarter.

I shrug my shoulders as I slip into the cold tub. "Pissed."

Alex shakes his head at me. "No shit, Sherlock."

I glare at him. "I played like shit. Do you really need me to break it down for you?"

"So grumpy." Alex laughs.

"I just got my game back, and that out there was a joke." I point toward the field.

"Statistically speaking, you're unlikely to win every game. We'll rally next week."

I rest my head against the metal of the tub, breathing through the freezing cold. "It's worse when you've been watching on the sidelines for the first half of the season and not contributing. How many more games could we have won if I was out there?"

"Hey." Alex slaps my arm. "You can't control everything. We all know that guy is a nasty player. Focusing on the what-ifs isn't going to do you any good."

I roll my eyes. "I've heard it all before."

It's hard to keep the disdain out of my voice. I keep thinking of everything that I did differently before this game.

"We'll get 'em next week." Alex says on his way out of the training room.

Maybe I shouldn't have called Tenley. Shouldn't have had sex with her. Granted, I haven't played in crappy weather like this since I got back, but this one stings.

No matter what coach says, I feel like I let my team down. Maybe if I made those field goals, we wouldn't have had to throw the ball as much. And that wouldn't have led to those picks.

I have to shut down these errant thoughts. It's not going to do me any good to spiral. I'll watch the film this week and we'll regroup.

And until then, I know I have someone who will help me through it.

Tenley. My light at the end of the endless tunnel that was today.

Chapter Twenty-Six

TENLEY

The click of the apartment door wakes me from my spot on the couch. The faded lights of the city cast a low light in the living room.

Jackson drops his bag by the door, a hard sound leaving his lips.

"Hey." My voice is quiet.

His eyes find mine. "Hi."

Walking over to me, Jackson drops down beside me. He looks worse for the wear tonight. "Sorry about the game."

"I don't want to talk about it." The words are far more bitter coming from him than I thought they would be.

"It wasn't your fault." I rest my elbow on the back of the couch, my hand on his shoulder offering some strength. The agitation coming from him is palpable.

Shock colors his handsome face. "I didn't say it was."

"I know." I pull my hand back, as if burned. "But I know how your mind works."

"You're not an expert on all things Jackson."

"I wasn't claiming to be." I'm not sure who this Jackson

is, but he's not the man I've come to know and love these last few weeks.

"I'm allowed to be upset that we lost the game."

"And I didn't say you couldn't be. But I'm not going to let you be rude to me about it."

"Well you make it sound like it was my fault," he growls.

I throw the blanket on my lap onto the floor. "I waited up to make sure you were okay after the game, and I literally told you that it was *not* your fault. But if you're going to act like this, then I'll see you tomorrow after work."

Instead of retreating to the safety of his room, I head to the guest room where I spent my first few weeks here. I've never experienced this side of Jackson, and it's not one I like.

Crawling under the cool sheets, I try to quell the simmering emotions just below the surface.

With this loss, Jackson's emotions are on a hair trigger. I know Jackson. I've been with him this entire season. Does he really think that I don't know where his mind goes after a loss?

People are quick to place the blame on everyone else's shoulders. Not Jackson. Jackson always takes it on himself, trying to figure out what he did wrong and how he can get one better for the next game.

Tears sting my eyes. It's late and I'm tired. I don't want to be annoyed with Jackson, but I am. Maybe this is the dark side of loving an athlete. Having to deal with all of their moods when things don't go exactly right. This last week has been long. The sportscasters have been focusing on the gossip surrounding Jackson and Rachel, and I hate it. I just want things to go back to how they were before the article came out.

A sick feeling washes over me as I pull the comforter up

and will sleep to come. Hopefully a good night's sleep will wash away these icky feelings Jackson has left me with.

THE SOFT PATTER of rain on the window wakes me before my alarm.

A gloomy day to match my mood.

Showering and getting ready faster than usual, I don't want to risk running into Jackson this morning. My emotions are close to the surface, and I don't want to get into it before school.

Luck isn't on my side today. Jackson is sitting in the kitchen, studying game film, when I make my presence known.

"Morning." He doesn't turn to look at me. "I made you some coffee."

"Thanks." I grab the travel mug sitting next to the pot and pour myself a cup.

Awkwardness filters through the air. Jackson doesn't acknowledge me beyond a pot of coffee. It's like we're back at square one, and I don't know how to act around him.

"Will you be home for dinner after practice?" I ask, breaking the stilted silence.

"Should be." He takes his own sip of coffee, not looking at me.

"If you will be, let me know and I can pick something up on my way home. We've got talent show practice after school, so I'll be late."

"Sure."

The short, clipped answers push me over the edge.

"Is this really how you act after you lose a game?" Frustration seeps into every word.

"You accused me of losing the game." His voice is harsh.

"No. I told you it wasn't your fault. There's a big difference, Jackson."

"Well it didn't feel good, Tenley." Hard eyes pierce through me.

"Next time I won't even talk to you after a game then. It's not my fault you lost either."

"Maybe if I wasn't distracted." His words aren't as quiet as he hoped.

"Wow."

That gets his attention. "Look, Tenley, I'm sorry, okay? That game sucked and we weren't ready. I have a process I go through after a loss, and I've never had to have someone around for it."

I grab my bag that's sitting on the island. "Good to know. I guess I'll just stay at my place then and let you work your process."

"C'mon. Don't be like that." He reaches for my hand, but I dodge out of the way.

"I wouldn't want to be a distraction to you." I throw his words back at him. "When you've worked through it, then we can talk."

I slam the door behind me with more force than necessary. As I walk through the lobby of Jackson's building to get to my car, the dreary day matches the gray in my chest.

I never thought Jackson would act like that. And to be the recipient of it? It feels pretty miserable.

Is this what football does to the man I love?

Because I didn't sign up for this.

Chapter Twenty-Seven

JACKSON

Nothing is going right today. We're down 24-10 in the third quarter. One measly field goal from me and that's it. LA has been playing lights-out football today. They were the underdog. We were supposed to win this game handily.

Instead, we're getting our asses handed to us. And everyone is feeling it. The fans in the stadium are getting restless as the offense is stopped on third down. Again.

"Still plenty of time, boys. Keep those chins up."

Our coach is trying to keep the energy up on the sidelines as our punter races onto the field. The crowd noise dulls to a low roar. Gray skies have made for a gloomy game. Almost like the weather matches our play.

It's been a long week. Things with Tenley have been strained, and practice wasn't great. The noise around Rachel's asinine article has finally died down. Probably because Alex was out from practice most of the week. It shows in his play today. Usually we bounce back after a hard loss, but not this week. It's like we're playing with anchors around our legs. The simplest plays are hard to execute today.

I sip on water as the defense strings together a few good plays, stopping them on third down.

"Nice job, Knox." I hold my fist out for him. He returns it with a shrug.

"Need to get offense going now."

Alex is going up and down the sidelines, motivating his line to get going. He's one of the best captains I've ever seen. People respect him and want to put themselves on the line for him. Everyone that's ever played for him loves him.

Between Colin and Logan, they're helping Alex execute the plays. Logan has a quick burst down the middle and ends up on LA's side of the field.

The spark is snuffed out just as fast. Getting stopped on the thirty-eight yard line, I'm summoned to the field.

I zone out the crowd noise as I line up. I tap my toe to the turf, letting my arms hang loose. Nodding to my holder, he calls for the ball.

Everything happens in slow motion. LA's guy jumps offside, sending everyone into a frenzy. As my leg connects with the ball, he gets a piece of me. It sends me into the grass at an awkward angle. My knee takes the brunt of the force and the pop is felt immediately.

"Fuck!" I shout, cradling my knee. I hear whistles being blown as my long snapper kneels next to me.

"Are you okay?"

"Do I look like I'm okay? Fuck!"

I don't care what I'm shouting because the pain is worse than the first time. It feels like someone shoved a hot iron inside my knee and twisted it around.

He steps back as the trainers make their way onto the field. They start maneuvering my knee, and any way they pull it hurts.

"Please stop. For the love of God, stop." I squeeze my eyes shut against the tears that threaten. My stomach is in knots at the amount of pain I'm in.

"Are you able to walk off the field?" They bend my knee, and it takes everything I have not to puke all over the field.

"Radio for the cart."

I flop back down onto the field, taking in the quiet stadium around me. Only one thought rolls through my head.

Not again.

Tenley

MY STOMACH IS in my throat as I watch Jackson get carted off the field. Sure, he's taken a beating playing before. You can't play football without your body taking a hit. But it's never been this bad.

"He's going to be okay." Gabby wraps an arm around me. Jackson gave me two tickets for the game this week, so she's my plus one.

"What if he's not? He just got back to playing." My mind goes to the worst-case scenario.

The game continues with LA taking the ball. I can't focus. What if Jackson's injury is more serious this time? Did he aggravate his knee? How's he feeling?

The swirling feeling of dread in my gut doesn't help.

"Excuse me, Miss Rhodes?" Someone dressed in team gear comes up behind me in the family suite.

"Yes?" I stand, spinning around to face them.

"Do you want to see Jackson?" I nod furiously. "If you'd follow me, we can take you down to the training room."

"Oh God."

"It's going to be okay. Can I come with her?" Gabby wraps an arm around me as she talks with the team rep.

"Yes. But we can't let you in the training room."

"That's fine. Can I see him now?" I'm ready to get moving. I can't imagine what is happening if they're bringing me down to the locker room.

We follow her through the bowels of the stadium, listening to the crowd, not knowing what's happening. I couldn't focus on the game if I wanted to. My only thought is getting to Jackson and making sure he's okay.

"Right through there. We'll be waiting here when you're done." I get a nod indicating it's okay to go in.

"It'll be okay, Tenley." Gabby gives me a squeeze before I push open the door.

My eyes are magnets to Jackson. His uniform is off, and a bag of ice is wrapped around his leg. "Oh my God. Are you okay?" I rush over to him, reaching out to touch him, but stop. His shirt is drenched in sweat, clinging to him like a second skin.

"Do you think I'm okay?" Bitterness drips from his voice.

I ignore his jab. "What did the team doctor say?"

"That I need to go to the hospital to get some scans so they know the extent of the damage done."

I swallow, my mouth drier than the Sahara. "What do they think happened?"

"You saw what happened," Jackson snaps.

"I saw the hit. But what did the doctors say?" I try to keep my voice level. Jackson doesn't need me getting upset with him.

"ACL." Jackson's jaw is hard. His eyes show nothing but anger. It can't be directed at me, can it?

This time, I rest my hand on his arm. "Let's just wait and see what the doctors say."

"Do you think it's going to be good news?" Jackson moves his arm out from under my touch, crossing his arms over his chest. "My knee is fucking throbbing, Tenley! It's not going to be good. Fuck!"

I jump back at his shout. I keep my mouth shut, not wanting to say anything to further upset him. I've never seen Jackson like this. Not after the loss last week. Not even when he first injured his knee.

I'm fast learning that Jackson has multiple sides when it comes to football. Sides I don't really like.

"Alright, Jackson." Someone, I'm only assuming the doctor, comes into the small room. "We're going to get you over to the hospital to see what we're working with and where we'll go from there."

Jackson grunts a response.

"Do you want to go with him?" the doctor asks me.

"Sure—"

"She doesn't need to be there," Jackson cuts me off. He's not looking at me.

"Then I'll be back in a few minutes. Hang tight." The doctor claps him on the shoulder before leaving.

"You can go home, Tenley. I'll call you later."

The thin thread of control I have on this situation snaps. "Then why did you want me to come down here?"

Jackson's eyes spin around the room, looking at everything but me. "I didn't ask for you to come down here. The team figured I'd want you down here."

"Let me come with you. If it's bad news, let me be there for you." I try appealing to him.

"I don't want you there! I've never needed anyone there before."

"That's sad, Jackson." My voice quivers. The man in front of me is breaking before my eyes.

"Yeah, well, it's the truth. This sport has been everything to me, even when people left."

I shake my head. "Football can't be everything."

"That's where you're wrong, Tenley." I hate how he sounds. Like someone I don't even know. "Football has been my whole life, long before you ever came into the picture. Football, not you." He leans back on the table, covering his face, oblivious to the blow he just delivered. Tears well in my eyes, but I fight them. Whoever this person is in front of me doesn't deserve them.

"I never asked to be your whole life, Jackson. I just want to be a part of it."

"Yeah?" He moves his hands, the hard look in his eyes something I've never seen. "Look where that got me. Injured, again, and probably needing surgery."

I clutch my hands to my heart, trying to hold the broken shards in. This is not the boy next door that I fell in love with. "So it's my fault that player ran into you as you were kicking?"

"If I wasn't so focused on you and how you were handling this whole Rachel and football situation, I would've been more concerned with my rehab. My knee would be stronger and it wouldn't have torn again. You're a distraction I can't afford, Tenley."

I laugh, an angry, caustic laugh. "A distraction? That's really how you see me? Who was the one to take you to rehab? Make sure you didn't move your leg when you weren't supposed to? Who helped you with your workouts?" I jab my finger at my chest, my voice rising now, unable to keep my emotions in check. "That was me. You would've hurt yourself a lot sooner if I wasn't there for you."

"So it's my fault then?" Jackson sits up, anger rolling off him.

"It's no one's fault!" I scream. "You can't control what happens. Look what happened to the player for Arizona who tore the same ACL again. God, you're such...an asshole right now!" The word slips out before I can pull it back, but I mean it. Jackson is acting like a self-righteous asshole.

"I don't need you here."

"Fine. Then I'll see you back at your place, I guess." I turn to leave, but his voice stops me.

"No."

"No?"

Jackson shakes his head at me. "I don't need you or anyone. I'm better off on my own."

The cold, calculating tone of his voice pierces my chest, finally spilling the broken pieces of my heart.

"If you truly believe that, Jackson, then I feel sorry for you."

"Then it's a good thing I don't need you."

I hold it together as I leave the stadium. As I drive through town. As I park my car in the garage. As I stumble through my house to the living room. But when I collapse on the couch, anguish overwhelms me. The loss of the boy I love consumes me. A pain I've never felt threatens my very essence. Tears burn hot down my face. I no longer have the safety of Jackson's arms to make the hurt go away.

I left my heart back at the stadium, and I don't know if I'll ever get it back.

Chapter Twenty-Eight

TENLEY

"Miss Rhodes?" Bobby tugs on my pant leg from where I'm standing at the board.

"What's wrong?" His blue eyes look confused.

"Where are all the football players today?"

I turn my eyes back to the board, taking a steadying breath. "Well, they couldn't come today because they have a big game this weekend."

"Aren't all the games big?" He cocks his head to the side. His sweet innocence brings a smile to my face.

"You're right. But this far into the season, it's hard for them to come visit. Maybe after the season."

Bobby shrugs his shoulder before going back to the reading corner. My eyes well with tears as I focus on writing letters on the board.

Every day this week has been a struggle. Mountain Lion pride is strong throughout the city. Every time I see the black and yellow, I have to look away. It all reminds me of Jackson. Of the way he so callously threw me aside.

No matter what I do, I can't wash the image of his eyes when he was in the training room at the stadium out of my head. It was not the man I knew growing up. The man that held my heart in his hands. I didn't even recognize that person.

"Ready to work on our talent show performance?" Ashley's voice startles me, breaking me out of my spiraling thoughts. With the winter holidays almost here, we've shifted our schedule to accommodate the upcoming talent show.

"Yes." Clapping my hands, I bring everyone's attention to me. "Who's ready to go to the gym and practice our talent show routine before some free time?"

Excited shouts greet my ears as we corral everyone into a semistraight line. Kids chatter on our way down, and as soon as we hit the gym, everyone goes running off in different directions.

"Okay everyone! Find your spot and I'll get the music started. If you get lost, just look to your friends around you."

I plug my phone into the speaker system, a kids' song echoing through the open space. Ashley and I try to help, but kindergartners just want to do their own thing.

"At least their parents already bought the tickets to come." Ashley laughs beside me.

"They'll be the cutest bunch to kick off the talent show."

"How are you holding up?"

I don't take my eyes off the practicing students. "I'm fine."

Ashley snorts next to me. "You're about as fine as a woman who just got dumped in a rom-com. I'm surprised you're not at home binging and crying into a tub of ice cream."

"More like a bottle of wine," I mutter.

"Have you talked to him?"

I shake my head as the song comes to an end. "That was great, everyone! One more time, and then you can play for a little bit. I know your families will be so excited to see you perform next week!"

I repeat the song and sit on a chair in front of them, doing everything I can not to wallow in my own sadness. "If he wanted me, he would've reached out. He said it himself—he doesn't need me."

"I saw the two of you together. You were made for one another. He's just scared of how much he loves you."

"He said I was a distraction, Ash." My voice wobbles. "That's not love."

"Oh sweetheart." She links her arm through mine, resting her head on my shoulder. "What man knows what's good for him? He's just scared because his future was a lot less clear after getting injured."

"Well, I can tell you what it doesn't involve, and that's me."

"You're just hurt. He'll come to his senses."

I chew on the corner of my lip, trying to quell the growing tears. Instinct has been screaming at me to pick up the phone and check on him. I wanted to check the Sports News Weekly website to see if they had any updates on his knee, but I couldn't. If I didn't hear it from Jackson, I didn't want to know. If he didn't care enough to tell me how he was, then I wouldn't go looking.

"And what if he doesn't? What if he doesn't come to his senses and there's no future for us?" My voice finally cracks, a tear sliding down my cheek. "What if Jackson was only supposed to be my past?"

The song ends, and without having to be told, all the students start running around and playing.

Ashley leans closer, whispering into my ear, cautious of

our surroundings. "Then you drink a bottle of wine and find a rebound."

My chest aches at the thought. I don't want a rebound. I've loved Jackson since I was fourteen years old. He's been in my life since we first walked to school together. The thought of him not being in my life is too hard to bear. But it's my new reality.

"Let's start with the wine. I'll let you know if I'm ready for a rebound."

Chapter Twenty-Nine

JACKSON

"Jackson. How ya feeling today?" Coach asks, walking into his office and sitting down at his desk.

"I've been better," I grumble. The crutches I've been hobbling around on all week lean against his desk.

He steeples his fingers in front of him, looking at the paperwork on his desk. No doubt it's the update from the team doctor on how my knee looks. I've been trying to prepare myself for this meeting, but it's not exactly a fun one.

"I know this isn't what you want to hear, but you're done for the season."

If my knee wasn't in a brace and could support my weight, I would've exploded out of the chair. "There's still time left in the season! I can still rehab it and come back. You can't put me on IR!"

Injured reserve. The two worst words to tell any football player.

"Son, it's for your own good. I don't want you to risk overdoing it and permanently injuring yourself. This game isn't worth it."

I shake my head, trying to keep my anger at bay. "But it is! This game is everything to me."

"Jackson." Coach stands, walking around his desk and sitting on the edge in front of me. "This game can't be everything to you. It *shouldn't* be everything to you."

"But isn't that what you want? Dedicated players?" I run a hand through the scruff on my chin. It's grown in thick. When I finally worked up the energy to shave, all I could think about was Tenley.

Her gentle touch. Her fingers caressing my face. The way she looked at me like I hung the moon.

I crushed the razor in my fist.

"Dedicated, yes. But I don't want you putting your life on the line for the game."

"Fuck." I lean back in the chair, staring at the popcorn ceiling. There are still a few weeks left in the season, and now, I wouldn't be on the field. Up until this season, I'd been healthy. I'd never taken a hit like the one I did in training camp. "Figures. I've never been injured before, and now I get injured twice in one season."

Coach claps a hand on my shoulder. "Did I ever tell you about my playing days?"

I shake my head, not sure if I'm ready to hear this story.

"Very first game of the season and we were playing Cincinnati. It was an out route, something I could've done in my sleep. But when I went to turn, I popped my Achilles and I was done for the season. Not a single person touched me."

"Shit. I don't think I ever knew that."

He shrugs his shoulder. "It's the life of the game. Had surgery and rehabbed it and came back again the next year."

"Did you win the Super Bowl?"

He laughs at me, shaking his head. "Wouldn't that have been a storybook ending? But no, I never won it as a player."

My chest deflates, releasing a long breath. "Is this the inspirational part where you tell me if I never make it to the big game, I'll be okay?"

He heaves out a sigh, sitting in the chair next to me. "No. It kind of sucked never winning the Super Bowl. But at the end of the day, I had other things that meant more to me than the game."

"What kind of other things?" I ask, prepping myself for the answer that I know is coming.

"A family. I had two young kids at home at the time, and even though I never made it to the Super Bowl, every time I came home, I felt like the damn MVP."

I smile, but it quickly fades at thinking what I might have lost. Having Tenley with me, even though we were only ever truly together for a few months, I felt more settled than I ever did with Rachel. Her bright smile and love of life were infectious. My entire apartment still smells like her, like it misses her too and isn't ready to let go.

"Football has been my entire life for as long as I can remember. It's kind of hard to make peace with the fact that I might not ever get a chance to win a ring."

"Do you know how hard it is to win a Super Bowl?"

I don't answer.

"At the beginning of training camp, there are almost three thousand hopefuls wanting to make a team. Any team. Three thousand, Jackson. Then we have to weed the team down to fifty-three. Then you have to gel as a team. And win. And what if you get injured? Cut? Traded? It's a seventeen game season. And then you have to go win another four games in the playoffs, three if you're lucky enough to get a bye. That's about a..."—he stops to think—"a three percent chance of winning a Super Bowl."

My head hangs in shame.

"There's nothing wrong in wanting to win the Super Bowl, son. But it can't be everything. You have to find something that means more than football. Something that you love so much that the thought of not having it would be worse than never playing another snap again."

Tenley fills my thoughts. Images of her laughing, dancing with her, cooking with her. The way she always looked at me. The way she cared for me. And the utter heartbreak when I told her to leave.

"What if I already had it and lost it?" All my pent-up anger was aimed at Tenley. I hated that I took it out on her, but she was there. Every day without her has been hell. A hell of my own making that I don't know how to climb out of.

"Jackson, whatever you did, I don't think it's bad enough to not come back from. You just have to fight like hell to get the things you love back."

Chapter Thirty

JACKSON

"You're a sight for sore eyes."

Alex's voice carries through the locker room. Practice has long been over for the team, but I haven't left. With my locker being cleared out, I wasn't ready to leave this place behind yet. Alex is surrounded by our other captains, Colin and Knox.

"I thought I could sneak in and out of here."

"Injured reserve sure makes you grumpy." Knox holds up a bottle of bourbon in his hand. "Figured this might help take the edge off."

"You're a dick." I hobble over on crutches and grab the bottle from him. Taking a hearty swig, it burns all the way down.

"Shit luck, Fields." Colin's hands are stuffed in his pockets. "How are you feeling about the whole thing?"

Instead of snapping at him, I take a minute. I've already pissed off Tenley; I don't want to add to the list.

"Honestly? I don't know. I don't want to be on injured reserve, but here I am." I wave a hand down my busted leg.

"At least you have Tenley." Alex takes his own swig of bourbon before passing it to Knox. I grab it before he can and take a shot.

"Not anymore."

All three of them groan in unison. "What the fuck did you do, man?" Knox asks.

"Why do you assume it was me?"

Colin quirks a brow at me. "Oh, I'm sorry. Are we supposed to assume that the brightest ray of sunshine did something to leave your sorry ass?"

I take another swig. I'm Ubering home anyway, so might as well.

"I might have taken everything that happened this week out on her."

"You didn't." Alex's tone is harsh. "It couldn't have been that bad, could it?"

"I might have told her she was a distraction and caused this to happen."

"Fuuuck." Knox winces away from me. "You really stepped in it."

"I was just so angry." I run a hand through my hair. "Football has been my entire life for so long, and with the thought of it being taken away, I lost it."

"I feel like there is a valuable lesson in here." Colin aims a smile my way that I don't return. My mood has been in the toilet this week.

"And what might that be?" I drop down to the bench, not being able to stand on my leg anymore.

"That maybe you shouldn't have conversations when you're in a lot of pain."

I don't blink. "Thank you for that wise wisdom, Sherlock. It's no wonder you don't have a girlfriend."

For the briefest of moments, I see a flare of something cross his face, but it's gone just as fast.

"What Colin is trying to say," Alex cuts off any further argument from him, "is that words were said in the heat of the moment. It's nothing that can't be undone."

"You weren't there."

I couldn't see past my own anguish that day. I was so bitter that my life's goal might have been taken away from me, that I lashed out at the only person to ever stick around. Why would she want to come back to me when I've been nothing but hot and cold with her?

"Jackson, for as long as I've known you, I've never seen you happier than you've been these last few weeks. You've always been kind of a grumpy ass. But Tenley made you happy. We all saw it." Alex drops down on the bench in front of me. "Are you really going to let that slip away?"

My eyes meet his, and there's a pain there. The four of us have never been ones to sit around and talk about our feelings. These are the only guys I would clue in to what I'm feeling.

Every single memory, good or bad, over the last thirteen years has been wrapped up with Tenley. Could I really live my life without any new memories of the woman I love?

A small smile tugs at the corner of my lips.

"That's the face of a man who isn't ready to roll over." Colin claps me on the shoulder. "So how are you going to win her back?"

The smallest comment from Tenley last week has my brain working on overdrive. "I have an idea. And I need your help."

Chapter Thirty-One

TENLEY

"Everyone did great! I am so proud of you." I give high fives to all my students around me. "Now we're going to go out and watch everyone else, okay? Cheer nice and loud."

Eager faces nod back at me as we file into the gym to watch the rest of the performances in the talent show. Once the class is all situated, I go and stand next to Ashley.

"They looked so cute up there."

I give her a huge smile, one of the first genuine ones I've had in weeks. "Any time kindergartners do anything, it's cute."

"Well, they could have just stood there, and it would've been great."

A few kids go up to start singing, and I lean against the wall. The last two weeks have been exhausting. Sleep hasn't come easy. I've been running on fumes. "I just wish Jackson could have seen them."

"He'll come to his senses."

I can only shake my head. "I'm really not holding out

hope at this point, but I know the kids would've loved to have had him here."

"Umm, are you sure he wasn't here?"

My brows pinch together in confusion at her question. "I'm positive he wasn't here."

Ashley nods in the direction of the stage, Jackson standing front and center.

"What in the world?" I whisper.

He clears his throat, before speaking into the microphone. "Hi everyone. Some of you might know me, but I'm Jackson Fields, and I'm a kicker for the Denver Mountain Lions."

"It's Mr. Jackson!" I hear Lily screech from her spot in the front row. Jackson waves down at her.

"Go Mountain Lions!" a parent calls from the stands.

Jackson laughs nervously. "Thanks, man. But today, I'm here to tell a story."

"What is he doing?" An uneasy feeling settles in my stomach as I watch him up on stage.

"Just watch," Ashley shushes me, eyes fixed on the stage.

"Once upon a time, a very long time ago, there were two friends."

The curtain pulls back, and two of the players from the team are on stage standing next to one another. Everyone in the audience breaks out into laughter. "They lived next door to each other and were best friends."

"Oh my God." My voice is quiet, my fingers coming to my lips to watch this play out.

"But one friend didn't realize the other friend liked him, so he decided to…"—Jackson pauses—"hold hands with another friend." Colin crosses the stage and takes what I'm only assuming is supposed to be Jackson's hand.

"Do we really need to hold hands?" he hisses at Jackson.

"Shut up and hold my hand," Alex, the team's quarterback, says as he grabs Colin's hand.

The entire audience is in a fit of hysterics watching this scene. But I know exactly what is going on.

"The boy and his other friend held hands for a long time. But the other friend was sad because she really wanted to hold hands with her best friend."

Knox, a huge hulking man who is supposed to be me, looks on sadly. "One day, way into the future, the boy stops holding hands with the girl." The two players stop swinging their hands together and Colin leaves the stage.

"The boy hurts himself and his friend helps take care of him."

Everyone is watching the stage, but I can only look on as Jackson tells our story. "When they realized they both really liked each other, they started holding hands."

Knox and Alex link hands, looking at each other like they don't know what is going on.

"Why is there so much hand-holding?" Ashley whispers.

"We're in a school."

"Oh, right."

"The boy really likes this girl, but he wasn't very nice to her." Knox rips his hand out of Alex's and goes to pout in a corner.

"I wouldn't say I pouted in a corner," I mutter.

Jackson's eyes lock on mine. The nerves swelling in my stomach are huge. I press a hand to try and contain them. "The boy didn't realize what he had until it was too late. And so now, he's hoping that his friend will want to hold hands again with him. Maybe forever."

My stomach is down near my feet as we stare at each

other. It's like we're the only two people in the room. Even from this far away, I can see the regret in his eyes.

"So, uh, yeah. Thanks for letting me crash the talent show," Jackson mutters and walks off the stage to a round of rowdy applause. Alex and Knox each take a bow before following him off stage to even more cheers.

"You have to go talk to him." Ashley grabs my arm, but my feet are glued to the floor.

"And say what?" My mouth is sandpaper as I process everything I just saw.

"I don't know, how about you love him and forgive him?" Ashley rolls her eyes at me. "You can't just stand here and ignore him. That might have been the cutest thing I've ever seen."

Giving me a light shove, Ashley squeals as I walk toward the back of the stage. It's a hotbed of activity. Students run around getting ready for their performances, while teachers and volunteers are trying to shake hands with the players who are here. A hand reaches out and grabs me, pulling me behind the ropes that operate the curtain.

"I was hoping you'd come back here." Jackson's words are whispered as I gaze at him. Up close, he looks tired. Bags sit under his eyes, and there's a tightness to his shoulders that wasn't there before.

"How'd you manage to get in here?"

"I sweet-talked the principal." Jackson gives me a small smile. "Had to get some face time with you somehow."

"You could have called."

"Would you have picked up?"

A quiver pulls at my lips, as I shake my head. I cross my arms, steeling myself for what I'm about to say. "Why would I have picked up? You said I was a distraction." I can't hide the hurt from my voice.

"I know. And I'm sorry. God, Tenley, I've never been more sorry about anything before in my life." Jackson grabs ahold of my forearms, his touch setting my skin on fire. It's only been a few weeks, but I've missed his touch.

"How do I know you're sorry? You say you want to 'hold hands again' but I don't think I can put up with football Jackson every year or when the drama that is Rachel decides to come at you again. I can't take that kind of emotional whiplash."

"The team put me on IR." Jackson says it so matter-of-factly, that I can't hide the shock on my face.

I gasp. "Injured reserve? Was it that bad?" Jackson is the only person I can simultaneously be mad at, but also want to comfort in his time of need.

"I won't need surgery, but coach doesn't want to risk me coming back and doing any permanent damage. Had a real come-to-Jesus talk with him."

"And what was that about?"

Jackson takes my hands in his, pulling me into him. His chest brushes mine, and all I want to do is throw myself into his arms, but I'm still wary of what he is telling me.

"That football can't be everything. That he never won a Super Bowl as a player, and I have to find something that means more than the game."

I gulp down air, ignoring the chaos around us. "And did you find something that means more to you than the game?"

He nods. "I did. And I'm afraid I didn't treat her well. She was the most important person to me, and I cast her aside like she meant nothing. Used her as a punching bag when things weren't going right with my game."

I swipe angrily at a tear that escapes. "All she wanted to do was make sure you were okay."

Jackson cups my cheek, thumbing another tear away. "I

don't know where I would be without her. She is the only person that matters to me, and I treated her like she meant nothing to me. I will forever be sorry. I love her so damn much, and all I want to do is be with her. To dance in the kitchen with her. To carve pumpkins with her. To play stupid games with her."

I couldn't stop the smile if I tried. "Maybe even a few minutes in heaven with her?"

Jackson's smile is bright, just for me. "There will definitely be lots of minutes in heaven with her. As long as she decides to trust me with her heart again."

I wrap my arms around his neck, pulling him down to me. "It's only ever been yours."

"Thank God." Jackson closes what little distance there is between us, his kiss healing every broken part of my heart. It's a tame kiss, but I feel it everywhere. It lights up every cell in my body that has been aching for this man in the worst way the last few weeks.

I break the kiss but don't move away from him. "I've missed you."

"These last two weeks have been the worst of my life."

I rest a hand on his chest, feeling the steady beat of his heart. "How's your leg doing? I wanted to call you every day to check on you…" I don't finish the sentence. We both know what happened.

"It'll heal. Once I finally pulled my head out of my ass, I realized that if I lost you, I would never be whole again."

My heart fluttered in my chest at those words. "Then it's a good thing you came to your senses."

"As long as I have you, Tenley, everything else will be a bonus. I just need you."

I lay the sweetest, most gentle kiss on his lips.

"Then you'll always have me."

JACKSON - TWO MONTHS LATER

"We can't be late, Tenley. Are you almost ready?"

When she walks out of the hotel's bathroom, I've never seen her look more beautiful. With her short hair curled and a silver, sequin dress hitting just above her knees, it takes everything I have not to drag her back into the bedroom to show her just how much I love her.

"They can't start without us." Her smile hasn't faded all day. From the time we touched down here until now.

"Now I'm thinking we might be really late. Fuck, Tenley. You're gorgeous."

She spins as she makes her way over to me. "You don't look so bad yourself, handsome." She smooths a hand down my black jacket.

"How did I get so lucky to find you?" I wrap my hands around her hips, resting them just above her perfect ass.

"Maybe we should thank your parents for moving in next door." She drops an innocent kiss on my lips before stepping back. "God, even Rachel gets a thank you because she's the one who hosted that party."

I smile, taking her hand in mine as we leave the room and head down the elevator from the top-floor suite. "Who would've thought that we'd end up here after that night?"

I brush her hair off her neck, dropping a kiss there. She sinks farther into my hold as I wrap my arms around her.

"I still can't believe we're doing this."

I look up, finding her eyes in the mirrored glass of the elevator. "I'm about thirteen years late. I hope you can forgive me."

Tenley spins in my arms as the elevator dings. "We wouldn't have been ready before now. Let's go. I'm ready to get this show on the road."

She takes my hand, walking backward into the crowded hotel lobby.

It took me a long time to see the woman in front of me. I'm just thankful she still wanted me. Because what I feel for Tenley is unmatched. Being put on IR had given me a lot of time to think. I get to be home when she gets home. Every night when I go to sleep next to her and when I wake up to her, I have to pinch myself. I thank my lucky stars she took me back. These last months have been nothing but bliss.

Some days it feels like my heart could burst with how much I love this woman.

"Mr. Fields. Your limo is here."

The valet waves to the long black car awaiting our arrival.

"Someone went all out this evening." Tenley gives me a playful look as she gets into the car.

"What can I say?" I unbutton my jacket, taking a seat next to her. "You deserve it."

A bottle of champagne and two flutes await us. Tenley

pops the cork, sending a spray into the back of the car. Her laugh settles me. Holding out the two glasses toward her, I watch as she pours some in each.

"What are we toasting to this evening?" She kicks her legs over mine, settling into the seat as we take off down the Vegas strip.

"To you, Tenley. Thank you for never giving up on me. Thank you for always being there for me. For loving me. I don't want to think about what life without you would ever be like."

She clinks her glass to mine before moving in closer. "And after tonight, you will never have to know."

Tenley's smile is brighter than the strip that guides our way to the small chapel where our family is meeting us.

That day a few weeks ago had been just an average day. After the Mountain Lions had a tough road loss, Tenley was there, waiting for me to fall apart. I could see it written on her face.

But I didn't. Having her there with me made it easier. I could see that final piece of her trust lock into place. She could trust that I wouldn't lash out at her every time something went wrong with the game. That was the moment I knew. There wasn't a doubt in my mind that I wanted to make her mine.

"MARRY ME."

"*What?*" *She looks shocked.*

"*I love you, Tenley. And there isn't anything I want more in the world than to marry you.*"

"*We've only been together a few months,*" *she reasons.*

I pull her down onto my lap. "*So? Even though I didn't know it was you, I've loved the person who gave me that kiss since I was a scrawny fourteen-year-old. And there is nothing I want more than to marry you."*

Her smile grows as she drops her forehead to mine. "You're serious?"

"If I never play another down of football, my life will be amazing because I have you in it."

"Do you even have a ring?"

I pick Tenley up, carrying her into my room. "Do I have a ring?" I laugh, mocking her.

Dropping her on our bed, I go into the closet and find the small velvet box. Walking back into our room, I grin as she covers her face with her hands.

"I've had this since the day we got back together. And I'd get down on one knee if I knew I could get back up."

Tenley pulls me back down onto the bed beside her.

"I might have lost my way there for a little while, but with you by my side, guiding me, guiding us, we will always be better together. I love you, Tenley, and nothing would make me happier than getting to be your husband."

I snap open the box, revealing a simple round-cut diamond set on a yellow-gold band. Nothing flashy, just like her.

"Will you marry me?"

"Of course!" She throws herself into my arms, kissing every part of my face. "Yes! Yes! Yes!"

I exhale, more nervous than I realized I was. "Thank fuck." I pull the ring out, sliding it onto her finger.

"It's beautiful." She wiggles her fingers in front of her face. "But can I have one request?"

"Anything for you." I kiss her neck, wanting to celebrate this moment with her.

"Let's go to Vegas. I don't want to wait to officially be yours. We can fly our families out, but let's do it. No waiting."

I smile, tackling her to the bed. "That's the best idea yet."

"Where'd you go?" Tenley's hand on my cheek brings me back to her.

"Just thinking of the moment I asked you to marry me."

Gulping down the rest of her champagne, she gives me a smile that is meant for only me. "Easiest answer I've ever given."

I pull her lips to mine, tasting the bubbles on her lips. She easily opens to me, her tongue tangling with mine. Every time I'm with this woman, I get lost in her. In the feel of her lithe body on top of mine, of her hands running through the strands of my hair.

I swallow her moan as I run my hands up under the hem of her dress. Her hands come down on top of mine, stopping them in their tracks.

"Don't start anything you don't intend to finish, Mr. Fields."

"I fully intend on finishing everything I start tonight, soon-to-be Mrs. Fields."

"I love the sound of that."

The sound of the divider comes down. "We've arrived."

The limo stops outside the small chapel that Tenley found for us. Our families are waiting outside as the driver opens the door.

"About time you got here!" my mom says, walking up and wrapping me in a hug.

"Trust me, I've been waiting a lot longer for this than you have." My eyes stay on Tenley who is hugging her mom and dad. Her sisters and Gabby are waiting next to them.

"We're almost ready for you." The wedding planner

stands at the entrance to the small chapel. "Jackson, if you'll follow me, we'll let Tenley get ready."

"See you in there."

"See you in there," she parrots back.

We part in the lobby. Walking back to one of the small rooms, booming voices hit me. Colin, Alex, Knox, and Logan are all crowded around a table in the center of the room.

"What the hell are you guys doing here?"

"You really thought you could get married without us?" Colin is the first to walk my way. "Real classy, bro."

"The season just ended. I thought everyone would need time to decompress." The Mountain Lions didn't make the playoffs. It was a rough season, even harder when I couldn't help them win like I wanted to. But things happen for a reason. There's no way I'd be here tonight if I didn't have the season I did.

"And miss this? No way." Alex hands me a drink. "No place else we'd be tonight."

"There's still time to back out." Knox claps me on the shoulder, sliding up to my side.

"Fuck off. There's nowhere I'd rather be tonight." I knock his hand off me.

"Just making sure. Not sure why Tenley wants a grumpy son of a bitch like you, but you two seem happy together."

I couldn't stop the smile spreading on my face if I wanted to. The only place I'd be tonight is here. In a small chapel at the end of the Vegas Strip waiting to marry Tenley.

"I don't know why you'd want to tie yourself down to one woman. You could have any woman you wanted," Colin muses. "I could get any woman tonight on the strip without even trying."

"You'll eventually learn, Colin." Logan shakes his head at him.

"Why was I so happy to see you guys here?" I laugh.

"Okay, okay. Stop giving Jackson so much shit." Alex corrals the guys. "If I may, I'd like to make a toast."

Everyone stops and circles around me. Glasses are raised into the air.

"To Jackson. I know it's been a hard season for you, but I think you may have gotten the best deal out of all of us. I know you and Tenley will love and appreciate each other because of what you've gone through, and that you'll be able to tackle any problems you may face."

Knox snorts. "Tackle. Nice."

"Grow up, bro," Logan admonishes.

My eyes lock with Alex's and we laugh. I shouldn't have expected anything less. This is why I love these guys and am glad they're here. "Alright, alright. To Jackson."

"To Jackson." We clink glasses as the wedding planner pops her head into the velvet-lined room.

"We're ready."

I blow out a breath, nerves hitting me.

"We'll see you out there. Congrats, man." They all smack me on the back as I follow the woman out to take my place and await my future wife.

My Tenley.

My forever.

Tenley

"ARE YOU READY?" Gabby asks.

Standing in the back of the small chapel with my dad, butterflies are swarming my stomach. "Yes."

"Then let's get going."

The music starts and both my sisters and Gabby start their walk down the short aisle. My dad holds his elbow out to me and I latch onto it.

"You look beautiful, Tenley. I'm so proud of you, and I know that Jackson is the right man for you."

Tears well in my eyes. "I have a feeling I'm going to blubber my way through this."

"It just means you know you're doing the right thing." He drops a kiss on my cheek as the music changes and I start my own walk down the small aisle.

Jackson is waiting at the end. And even though I only just saw him a few moments ago, my heart is bursting with love.

I've been in love with this man for almost half my life. He gave me my first kiss. He was there for me during every major moment. And when he needed me most, I was right there for him.

All the while, our love for one another kept growing. It changed and evolved to what it is now. Something so deep, something so all-encompassing, that I don't know if I'd survive a day without him. Because this man means every-thing to me.

By the time I meet him at the end of the aisle, tears are rolling down my face. "Take care of each other," my dad whispers to us as Jackson takes my hand and pulls me to his side.

The woman before us launches into the wedding sermon, and Jackson keeps his eyes right on me. Growing up, I always thought I wanted a big ceremony with everyone I know in attendance. It turns out, all I need is my family and Jackson. Because they're all that matters.

"Now I believe you each wrote your own vows?"

Jackson nods, and she indicates for him to start.

"Tenley, I thought I knew exactly what my life was going to be like. Playing football and getting married along the way. Turns out, I knew absolutely nothing. Because ever since I met you, I was just waiting for our moment. You're it for me. As long as I have you in my life, I'll have everything I need. I love you more than anything in this life, and I will spend every day showing you just how much you mean to me."

I sniffle at his words, letting his love wash over me. "Jackson, I've been in love with you since you moved in next door. And even though we weren't together, I loved you from afar. And when I finally got to show you how much I love you, I didn't know someone could love like that. You make it easy to love you. There will be hard days ahead, but I know that as long as we're in this together, we'll be okay. Because all I need is you. I love you."

I love you he mouths back.

A tear escapes his own eye, and I reach up to wipe it away. We finish the rest of the ceremony before she tells us to kiss one another. Everyone in the small room whoops and claps as Jackson lays one on me.

It's the best kiss of my life. Sealing our love, our promise for the future, and everything we mean to one another. His smile when he pulls back has me leaping into his arms.

"To Mr. and Mrs. Fields."

"I love you, Mrs. Fields," Jackson whispers down to me.

"And I love you, Mr. Fields."

Jackson gives me another soul affirming kiss before we walk back down the aisle together.

Finally getting our forever after fourteen years.

The End

Want to see what Jackson and Tenley are up to? Keep reading to find out more…

Bonus Scene

JACKSON

"Fields, you coming out with us tonight?" Knox pipes up from the locker next to mine. It was our first day of organized team activities, OTA's, today, and as much as I want to hang with the guys, someone else is calling my name.

"Sorry man. It's the first day of summer break for Tenley and we're celebrating tonight."

"I wish we got summer break," Colin laments.

"Dude. We basically have summer break from February to June." Alex smacks him across the chest.

"Yeah, but summer break was the best. No school. Swimming. I wish we could go back."

"And on that note," I tug my t-shirt down, "I'm going home to see my wife."

"You are disgustingly in love," Knox chirps up.

I give him a saccharine smile. "Damn right I am."

Grabbing my bag, I hoist it over my shoulder and head out from the practice facility. Even though I have spent the last few weeks wrapped up in Tenley, I've missed her these last few hours.

Now that she finally has free time, I'm back at training.

But it feels good. My knee is strong. The trainers were nothing but careful with me since I was put on injured reserve, and I've never felt better.

Thankfully it's a quick drive through the city, the afternoon traffic not yet starting up. The elevator ride up to our floor is quick as I slide my key in the lock.

"You're home too early!" I hear Tenley yell from inside.

"I told you I'd be home by three."

Tenley slides in front of me, covering my eyes with her small hands. "It's only two. That's early."

"Why can't I be home?"

"Because I'm not done with your surprise." The *duh* is implied at the end of her sentence.

"What do you suggest I do until you're done?" I cover her much smaller hands with mine, bringing them down off my face. My eyes are tightly closed, not wanting to incur this woman's wrath.

"Go into the bedroom."

"I'm liking this idea." I waggle my eyebrows, not exactly knowing where she is.

"That's not what we're doing Jackson. Now, follow me."

Tenley tugs me toward her. I'd follow this woman anywhere.

My knees hit the back of the bed when Tenley tells me I can open my eyes.

"Hi there, handsome." Tenley's hands land on my shoulders.

"Mmm, hi there." I drag my hands up the backs of her legs, pulling her into me. Her soft scent overwhelms me. God, I love this woman.

"Can you give me just a few more minutes to get your

surprise ready?" Her forehead kisses mine, her breath hot against my lips.

"I need a kiss before you go," I whisper. "It's been too long without one."

"I saw you this morning." Tenley peppers my lips with kisses.

But I don't let her get far. I drag her back to me, sinking my teeth into her lush bottom lip. I'm ready to throw her on the bed and ravage her. I want to feel her heat around me and get lost in this woman.

Tenley has other plans. "No. You can't get carried away before I give you your surprise. I'll be right back."

She pushes me backward on the bed and runs out of the room. I watch her go, growling as need now pulses through me.

But when is it not? My need for this woman runs hot. I don't know what I did without her in my life, because I can't imagine her not being here with me.

My ball of sunshine strides into the room, a smile stretched across her face.

Tenley drops a box in my hands. "It's not much, but the mail was late today, but I think you'll like it."

She's sitting cross-legged on the bed next to me, clasping her hands. I tug at the bow holding it together and pull out a tiny jersey.

A onesie jersey to be exact. With my number and *Daddy* emblazoned on the back.

"Tenley…" I can't find the words. I turn to find tears in her eyes. "Does this mean what I think it means?"

"It does."

"We're having a baby?"

"We're having a baby!" Tenley tackles me to the bed. "I'm pregnant!"

"Holy shit!" I push Tenley's hair out of her face. I don't

know how I missed it before now. She's glowing. "When did you find out? I thought the test you took was negative."

Not long after we got married, we decided we didn't want to wait to start our family. We'd waited fourteen years to be together. We weren't getting any younger, and wanted kids like yesterday.

"I thought it was too. But I started feeling sick at work last week and knew something was off."

I roll us over, settling Tenley in the middle of the bed. My hand dips under her shirt, settling on her stomach. She doesn't look any different, but fuck, we're having a baby.

"Why didn't you tell me you were feeling sick?"

Her hand lands on mind. "Because I didn't want to get your hopes up."

My vision starts to blur as I bury my face in Tenley's neck. "Holy shit, Tenley."

I can't stop saying the words.

Tenley and I are going to be parents.

"You are going to be the best fucking mom out there." I trail kisses up her neck, nibbling her jaw as I work my way to her lips.

I swallow her laugh in a kiss, our tongues tangling.

"You know you're going to have to cut back on the cursing, right?"

My gaze locks on hers. "I guess you're going to have to teach me your tricks."

"What a hard job." She pulls me down for another kiss.

"I wonder what our kids will look like," Tenley says, dragging a hand down my arm and linking our fingers together.

"God, I want someone I can play football with. And that we can read to every night."

I look at the jersey again.

"I can't believe we're having a baby, Tenley. I don't think I ever imagined life could be this good."

"Well you better believe it, Mr. Fields, because it's going to get even better."

"I can't fucking wait, Mrs. Fields. I can't fucking wait."

Author's Note

Book 8 is out in the world!

The Denver Mountain Lions series is my love letter to football. Growing up in the Peyton Manning era in Indianapolis, you couldn't not love football. So when it came time to plan a new series, a sports romance was a no brainer! So the Mountain Lions were born.

Roughing The Kicker was an absolute joy of a book to write. I fell in love with Jackson and Tenley immediately, and instead of having their book be last in the series, I moved them to first in the series. Special shoutout to my travel bestie Rachel…who is not terrible like the Rachel in the book <3

There are so many people to thank, and I always worry that I'm going to miss someone…

To each and every author friend, who are too many to name, I can't thank you enough for your endless support! Without you, I wouldn't be where I am today!

To my Street Team…thank you for your loving on my books as much as I do!

To all the readers, bloggers, bookstagrammers, and booktokers...thank you for reading and taking a chance on my books! I couldn't do it without you.

About the Author

After winning a Young Author's Award in second grade, Emily Silver was destined to be a writer. She loves writing strong heroines and the swoony men who fall for them.

A lover of all things romance, Emily started writing books set in her favorite places around the world. As an avid traveler, she's been to all seven continents and sailed around the globe.

When she's not writing, Emily can be found sipping cocktails on her porch, reading all the romance she can get her hands on and planning her next big adventure!

Find her on social media to stay up to date on all her adventures and upcoming releases!

Also by Emily Silver

The Denver Mountain Lions

Roughing The Kicker

Pass Interference

Sideline Infraction

Illegal Contact

The Big Game

Dixon Creek Ranch

Yours To Lose - newsletter bonus story

Yours to Take - coming March 23, 2023

Yours to Hold - coming June 29, 2023

Yours to Be - coming August 24, 2023

Yours to Forget - coming November 16, 2023

Off the Deep End — A standalone, MM sports romance

The Ainsworth Royals

Royal Reckoning

Reckless Royal

Royal Relations

Royal Roots

Royal Ties

The Love Abroad Series

An Icy Infatuation

A French Fling

A Sydney Surprise

Get all my titles now:

www.ingramcontent.com/pod-product-compliance
Lightning Source LLC
Chambersburg PA
CBHW030813210726

48290CB00002B/563